Jackson just plum couldn't figure the woman out, and that was the truth.

"I don't date," Vanessa said.

"Okay."

"Like I said, I don't have time."

"Okay."

"But the flowers were beautiful."

"So you said."

During their one previous phone conversation, she'd been on the chilly side. When she'd first seen him tonight, she'd been surprised and, again, not pleased...at first anyway. Now, as she sat next to him in the car, he sensed some inner tightness slowly uncoiling. If she wasn't being exactly warm to him, she was, at least, treating him like a human being.

A human being who didn't date, he reminded himself. But dammit, he was still taken with her. He wanted her, and that was at the most primitive level, man to woman. Even in her no-nonsense navy-blue skirt and pale green blouse, she radiated enough sensuality to heat a small room.

Dear Reader,

Writers are sponges; we soak up all kinds of words and images, other people's stories and odd dreams. Sometimes I hate myself for this quality, especially when I'm listening to a friend pour her heart out, because although I'm appropriately filled with compassion and offer love and support, still there is that part of my brain that's wondering if I can use it in a book. It's sort of a vampire-ish quality, isn't it? The taking-in and ingesting that which is not mine, but someone else's.

This book, *One Cool Lawman,* is one of those. My dear friend Karen York (we've been buds since age fourteen) was telling me about this luncheon she'd attended the previous day. It was in honor of a woman from an impoverished childhood who had been an addict and prostitute, with two children from two different fathers. Somehow this woman had managed to get clean, get educated, get a real job with a future, and now had both children under her roof. The kids were doing great and so was their mother.

"Wow," I said to Karen. "What an amazing story." I thought to myself, is there any chance they'll let me write a heroine like that? I picked up the phone and called my editor, who said to go for it. So here it is. The idea may be straight from someone else's life, but I hope I wrote a piece of fiction that does honor to a remarkable, brave and inspiring true-life heroine.

Love,
Diane

Diane Pershing

ONE COOL LAWMAN

Silhouette®

Romantic

SUSPENSE

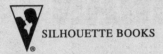

SILHOUETTE BOOKS

ISBN-13: 978-0-373-27536-6
ISBN-10:   0-373-27536-6

ONE COOL LAWMAN

Visit Silhouette Books at www.eHarlequin.com

Printed In U.S.A.

Books by Diane Pershing

Silhouette Romantic Suspense

While She Was Sleeping #863
The Tough Guy and the Toddler #928
Whispers in the Night #1337
Whispers and Lies #1386
One Hot Target #1458
One Cool Lawman #1466

DIANE PERSHING

For more years than she cares to disclose, Diane Pershing made her living as an actress and singer. She was extremely contented in these professions, except for one problem—there was way too much downtime, and she worried that her brain was atrophying. So she took up pen and paper and began writing, first for television, then as a movie critic, then as a novelist.

She wrote her first novel, *Sultry Whispers,* following the dictum to "write what you know," and it was about a voiceover actress who battled the male-dominated mindset of advertising agencies. There have been fifteen more sales since. Diane is happy to report that there is no more downtime in her life; indeed, with writing and acting—and teaching classes in both—she now faces the problem of not having enough time, which she says is a quality problem indeed. She loves to hear from readers, so please write to her at P.O. Box 67424, Los Angeles, CA 90067 or online at diane@dianepershing.com. You can also visit Diane's Web site at www.dianepershing.com.

To Alma L, for inspiring me with her story.
You are truly a miracle.

Chapter 1

Woman of the Year. She was being honored as Woman of the Year.

Unbelievable.

As she sat on the dais and heard the words of praise and admiration filling the church auditorium, Vanessa shook her head. Sure, she'd been warned about it beforehand—that all the fuss might make her feel exposed, vulnerable, raw, embarrassed, all of which it did—but what they hadn't said was that this small ceremony would make her feel like an impostor. Hearing herself spoken about as though she were one step removed from Mother Teresa, well, it just didn't sit well with her. Vanessa didn't feel that special, far from it in fact. She'd done what she'd done in order to survive. Period.

"...and we at A Single Voice agree," the speaker was

saying, "that Vanessa Garner's life is a success story, an inspiration to us all. A child of poverty and abuse, Vanessa lived on the mean streets of Los Angeles from her early teens, doing whatever she had to do to stay alive...."

Nervously Vanessa shuffled the index cards in her hand. Soon it would be her turn to get up there with her thank-you speech, and she just wanted it to be over.

"...Vanessa's mother married four times. Two of her stepfathers were abusive. She ran away from home to escape. She was fourteen at the time...."

Sure, she'd run away, and not only from the man who had taken her virginity in a violent act of rape and told her he'd be back for more. She'd also run away from the mother whose alcoholic haze prevented her from hearing her daughter's cries for help. She'd run away from the fear and the despair and the sense of hopelessness that permeated her home...and found a world even more fearful, one filled with so much despair that more than once she'd considered taking her own life.

Do not go there, she told herself, back to the memories and the pain. She'd gotten past it. This was now, not then.

To distract herself, Vanessa glanced sideways at the others on the dais, and she got smiles of warm encouragement back from city councilman Marvin Kahn, Reverend William Jones and her friend and lawyer, Shannon Coyle. But the last one, the cop, he didn't smile at all.

He was a big guy, dwarfing the bridge chair he sat on. Wearing his dress blues, arms crossed over his broad chest, his face an unsmiling stone mask, he didn't look at all happy to be here. He had close-cropped brown hair and a faint beard shadow, and from what she could tell, his biceps were huge. He was here on behalf of the local police precinct, and was a detective, if she remembered correctly. They'd been introduced briefly beforehand, and the minute she'd heard his faintly Southern accent, she'd known all she needed to know.

Way too much testosterone, she'd thought then and still thought. Probably enjoyed taunting street junkies. He sure wasn't the clean-cut, Junior Chamber of Commerce type that police departments usually had representing them at community relations events.

"…as is all too common with children on the streets," the speaker went on, "Vanessa got involved with drugs. It was a struggle to support herself and, later, her children. No one helped her, no one took care of her, no one parented her."

Vanessa shot a look at her kids, sitting there in the front row on either side of a beaming Aunt Lupe. A lot of what they were hearing today was sanitized, of course, but she'd told them about her past with drugs, mostly as a warning to them. Now she wondered how they were reacting to hearing about it in public. One by one she met their gazes with a smile for each: fourteen-year-old Shane, twelve-year-old Thomas and the baby, Katy, age six. They smiled back—even Shane, her oldest, who didn't smile much at all these days.

She felt her heart filling with that special mother joy. They were the reason she was alive, they were her reason to keep on living, the reason she was here today. Just looking at them made her feel better, made her nervousness ease up.

Absently her gaze panned the rest of the audience: not a large group, and no press, thank God. A Single Voice— the multiracial group of successful, wealthy women who genuinely cared about giving help to other women, those who were disadvantaged and decidedly *not* wealthy— preferred to do their work outside the spotlight.

"She tried to break her addiction many times over the years, but always fell short of success. Until that last time, over six years ago…"

Getting closer to speech time, Vanessa thought, clutching her index cards again, as her gaze swept over the rest of the audience: a few friends, some associates from work and two rows of sullen teenage girls from the Youth Authority, who were supposed to hear her story and be inspired by the tale of someone just like them who'd found a way out of the violence and poverty they'd all grown up with.

Would it have an effect? Vanessa wondered. Maybe, maybe not.

A sudden movement in the back of the room made her shift her eyes in that direction. A man had just walked in. There was something about him that looked…

She froze. No. Oh, please God, no.

But God must have been occupied elsewhere because her first impression was correct. A shiver of fear zipped up and down her spine at the sight of Romeo "Ray" Ortiz, drop-dead handsome, street smart and deadly. In a way, the catalyst for her presence here today, painful as that catalyst had been.

Three months before Katy's birth, Ray had beat Vanessa to within an inch of her life. Miracle of miracles, Katy had come out of it unharmed, but Vanessa still had occasional ringing in her ears as a reminder of his vicious attack.

And now he was here. Her heart thudded loudly in her chest. Why had he come?

He caught her looking at him, smiled in that smooth, self confident, cock-of-the-walk way Ray had. Then he took a seat in the rear of the auditorium, crossed his arms over his chest and sat back to enjoy the show.

Her heart rate sped up some more; she was finding it difficult to breathe. Was she about to have a panic attack? She hadn't had one in years, and it took all her strength to concentrate on slowing her breathing. Please no, she prayed silently. Not here. Not in front of her kids, Aunt Lupe. Not in front of everyone. Not on this very special day.

Jackson Rutherford, Detective First Class, wished he were wearing his aviator shades today because then he might be able to grab himself a little shut-eye during this thing. However, no shades. This might be Los Angeles, but even so, a cop in sunglasses was not the "look" the department preferred. He stifled a yawn. Damn, he was tired. Too many beers at the ball game last night, not enough sleep. He probably looked like hell, not that he cared.

He was grumpy and that was a fact. Didn't want to be here.

Bored, his gaze scanned the audience and stopped when he caught the entrance of a man in the rear of the auditorium. Jackson tried not to be obvious as he checked him out. The newcomer seemed familiar. Slick, tough, good-looking—almost pretty. Clothes a little too sharp, a little too show-offy, even though obviously expensive. Gold chain around his neck, a flashy gold watch on his wrist. A man on the other side of the law in some way, he was pretty sure.

Jackson didn't know if the sense of familiarity he was experiencing was about the type in general or specific to this man in particular. Had his mug shot been posted on the station bulletin board? He couldn't be sure, but if it had, it was something to do with drugs. Which happened to be Jackson's area of expertise.

The late arriver was leveling a steady stare at today's honoree. Vanessa something. Jackson hadn't paid much attention to the name when his partner, Sal, had begged him to fill in for him, last minute, so he could rush his expectant wife to the hospital. Jackson wasn't real nuts about doing community relations, especially when he'd planned to sleep in this morning, but he couldn't say no to his partner, now, could he? Which meant he'd had about ten minutes to shower, dress, and get his butt over here, so he'd missed a couple of details, like names.

He shifted his attention over to the woman being honored. She wasn't looking at the guy at the back of the room, not at the moment, but he was pretty sure she'd been doing just that. She seemed really tense. Could be stage fright, could be something else. He noted the clenched jaw, a slight flaring of the nostrils. Her chest, under the conservative suit jacket and blouse she wore, was heaving up and down pretty rapidly. Panic? Fear? Both?

Or maybe she was excited. By the entrance of the new guy in the back? Maybe he was her dealer, and maybe she was looking to get high as soon as this little ceremony was over. Maybe she wasn't as pure, as recovered, as *honorable* as the lady giving the speech was making her out to be.

Which would be a shame, Jackson thought. A damned shame. Beautiful woman like that. He'd noticed her the minute he'd hurried into the church auditorium right before the ceremony and someone had made quick introductions. Hell, you couldn't miss her. Some women radiated sensuality like gardenias gave off perfume. She was one of those. Even her speaking voice, smoky, throaty, the kind that you wanted whispering to you in bed, was a turn-on.

"…so by the time we at A Single Voice heard about her six years ago," continued the lady at the microphone, "Vanessa was the twenty-five-year-old homeless mother of three children and a recovering addict. With all that history, with all that pressure, others might have gone back to the streets, but not Vanessa. Others might have given up their children, but not Vanessa. Others might have given up on living, but not Vanessa. No, Vanessa wanted to learn, wanted to be self-supporting, wanted more for her children, and that fierce will to succeed led her to seek help, to find good child care, to work a full-time job while going back to school…"

Pretty amazing stuff, Jackson had to admit. If it was all true. Which it probably was, as he'd been told that award recipients from A Single Voice were vetted pretty thoroughly. Trying not to be obvious, once again he looked sideways to check her out.

Vanessa something was racially mixed, but hard to pin down. Some Eurasian, for sure. With a little Latina and just a smidgeon of African-American thrown in? Whatever it was, it worked. Skin a pale-gold color, blue-green eyes that tilted up at the ends and straight, jet-black hair pulled severely off her face and gathered at the nape of her neck in a tortoiseshell barrette. High, rounded cheekbones, a small nose with a flattened bridge, full lips, a long, graceful neck. More exotic than beautiful, she was dressed in a modest gray suit and white blouse, pearl studs in her ears, two-inch heels, nothing that would attract attention.

But it was like throwing a net over a peacock to try to hide its colors. Couldn't be done. The woman was sensual down to the bone, discharging invisible phero-mones into the air like an automatic BB gun.

"A born courtesan type," as his mama would say, sniffing through her nose with disdain.

Jackson had to smile. Wouldn't Mama hate it if she knew what he was thinking? Lillian Beauregard Ruther-ford, proud member of the Daughters of the Confed-eracy, would not like her only son being attracted to anyone not pure white and upper crust, preferably born below the Mason-Dixon line. Jackson and Lillian didn't agree on this little matter, nor on many others, such as what he should be doing with his life, which was one of the reasons he'd put twenty-five hundred miles between them by coming west all those years ago.

But still, his mama's voice was in his head, and it popped up at the damnedest times.

* * *

"…and that fierce will is why today Vanessa is the manager of a business with over twenty employees, the loving mother of three beautiful children who attend school and have friends and a home and food on the table every night of their young lives. That fierce will is why she is this year's recipient of A Single Voice's Woman of the Year Award. Ladies and gentlemen, please join me in honoring Vanessa Garner!"

She didn't know how she got through the next fifteen minutes. As though from a distance, she heard the warm applause, managed to stand, smile at the audience, took in the cheers and "You go, Mom!" from Thomas, and walked over to the podium. She thanked the speaker, thanked all the members of A Single Voice, then gave her short, carefully rehearsed speech.

As she did, one big chunk of her brain couldn't stop focusing on Ray. He was like a flashing neon sign in a starless sky. Why was he here? She hadn't heard from him since before Katy was born. Why now? What did he want?

After the ceremony, when she'd been congratulated and hugged and kissed, after she'd sent the kids off to the car with Aunt Lupe and told them she needed to go to the rest room and would join them in five minutes, after she'd washed her hands and applied new lipstick, she found out just what Ray wanted.

He was waiting for her in the narrow, deserted hallway outside the ladies' room, and the moment she exited the door, he grabbed her, clamped a hand over her mouth and dragged her into a small storage room off the hall. Shutting the door behind them, he flicked on the single overhead bulb. Music stands and janitorial supplies were crammed all together, leaving barely any space for her and Ray.

She struggled to get free, her voice muffled behind his hand, but he was strong.

"Hush, *chica*," he said in that rich, deeply hypnotic voice of his. "I'm not going to hurt you, so you don't have to scream or nothing. Okay?"

She nodded.

"I'm going to take my hand away. But you need to promise not to scream. Deal?"

When she nodded again, he removed his hand.

Trying to catch her breath, she stared at him wordlessly. He was still beautiful, with those large, melancholy brown eyes, caramel skin and black hair. The face of a poet, she'd thought in the beginning. The soul of a cruel devil, she'd known by the end. The only changes the years had brought were a few lines radiating from the corners of his eyes and a small soul patch beneath his bottom lip.

"What do you want, Ray?"

"What's this?" He grinned, his perfect white teeth shining like alabaster. "No 'Good to see you, Ray'? No hugs for your long-lost friend? It took me a long time to find you, you know."

She crossed her arms over her chest so he couldn't see that her hands were shaking. "Why did you?"

He stared at her for a moment longer, a look of speculation in his too-beautiful eyes. "You've grown up, 'Nessa."

"About time, I think. I'll be thirty-one in a couple of months."

"And still looking good enough to eat." He licked his sensual lips, lips that used to drive her crazy when she was younger and a lot stupider. Back when she'd had no idea there were options, a different kind of life than the one she was living.

"Not interested," she said flatly, pleased at how calm she sounded. "Again, what do you want?"

For a brief moment there was a flash of displeasure in his expression; it was the same look that used to precipitate one of his rages, rages that left her battered and bruised and wanting to die because there was no way out.

He didn't have that kind of power over her anymore, she reminded herself. She was long past feeling and acting like a victim. "Touch me and I will scream, Ray," she said, keeping her voice firm and steady, even though she was quaking inside. "There are a lot of people around."

He blinked, seemed taken aback. He wasn't used to her fighting him, wasn't used to Vanessa with claws. He grabbed her by the wrist, twisted her arm behind her back. "Don't push me, *chica*," he growled in her ear.

It hurt. She fought, twisted, tried to pull away. Tears of pain filled her eyes. There were no windows in the dusty storage room. The door was closed. No one would hear her if she screamed. Or if they did it might be too late. She shouldn't have baited him. She was a fool, a stupid fool.

Gasping with pain, she said, "I'm sorry, Ray," even though she hated hearing the words coming out of her mouth.

"You better be," he snarled, twisting one more time for good measure before dropping his hold on her.

She rubbed at her bruised wrist. "Just tell me, okay?" she sniffled. "What do you want?"

He shrugged easily. "It's simple. I want my kid."

"Excuse me?"

"What do you call her? Katy? She's half mine. I want her."

"What do you mean, you want her? You want—what? To see her? To visit her?"

"No. I want her to live with me. With us. With me and my wife."

"Your wife?"

"Yeah. I got married. Last year."

"Congratulations," Vanessa said automatically, then stifled a nervous laugh at how ludicrous that was. What she was thinking was *The poor woman.* Had he beaten her yet?

"Yeah, thanks." His smile was smug, preening; irony had always been lost on Ray. "She's pretty classy, my wife. From a good family. From back east. You know, from money." The expression on his face said *Look how far I've come.*

"Well, good."

"And, yeah, see, Sharon, she can't have any kids. So I told her I already have one. And so that's why I'm here."

Her eyes dry now, her pulse steadier, Vanessa stared at him in disbelief. He was something else, Ray was. He'd always had this way of not dealing with reality. If he didn't want to hear something, he didn't hear it. Simple. It didn't exist. Bad news? Someone else's pain? It was like he snapped his fingers and it was gone. Like that. He could talk himself into believing whatever made him happy. And obviously he'd decided he would find Vanessa, pop in and simply pick up his child.

Like walking down a grocery aisle and finding the right brand of tomato juice, putting it in his cart and going on his merry way.

Not this time.

"Katy lives with me, Ray," she told him. "And that's the end of the discussion." She reached for the doorknob, but his hand pulled the door shut before she got it partway open.

"You're not hearing me, *chica*."

"Yes, I am. Katy is mine."

"Mine, too."

"No." She knew she shouldn't challenge him but couldn't stop the words. "You planted the seed, that's it. And after the beating you gave me, she nearly didn't get born at all. So, no, Ray, I don't really think she's yours. You don't deserve her."

She saw the flaring temper, the way his jaw was working, and that automatic fear reaction started up inside her again. She fought it. It didn't matter what she was *feeling,* she reminded herself, only how she *acted.*

She held up a hand. "Don't, Ray. I mean it. Don't lay a hand on me."

"Or what, 'Nessa? Remember how it used to be? Remember my fists? What do you think you can do to me?"

At that moment the door flew open. The cop from the dais stood in the doorway, nearly filling the frame with his huge muscular physique. "It's not what *she* can do to you," he said slowly, drawing out each word with that hint of a Southern drawl in each of them, "it's what *I* can."

It was like a moment out of an action movie made from a comic book character, Vanessa thought wildly. A caped crusader appearing suddenly to save the day. She bit back another nervous giggle as an image formed in her brain, then changed. A caped crusader with sunglasses. Her hero had put on dark aviator shades, so you couldn't see his eyes. Why, she had no idea. Nor had she any idea how he happened to have been out in the hall, but she was really glad he had.

Ray was less so. His eyes slits, he barked, "Who asked you?"

"No one," the cop said easily, sounding almost folksy. "I was just strolling by and it sounded like someone was threatening someone. And, see, I'm not too nuts about people threatening other people. And when a man threatens a woman, I get real displeased."

"This is a private conversation, cop," Ray said dismissively. "Get lost."

The detective, whose name she wished she could remember, locked gazes with Ray for a moment before shifting his sunglasses-covered eyes to Vanessa. "Do you want me to leave, ma'am?"

Again she had to stifle a nervous giggle. Except for the dark glasses, now he was like a lone gunslinger in one of those old Westerns her mother used to watch on TV in the afternoons. With Vanessa cast as the sweet but feisty schoolmarm. All that was missing was a horse and a Stetson. He certainly had the six-shooter. Although not on him, from what she could tell.

Why was he here? When she'd been hastily introduced to the big, broad cop before the ceremony, her first impression had not been a positive one. With her history, she wasn't partial to the male sex, most especially male cops. And this one was so white bread he sparkled.

His initial reaction to her hadn't been all that positive, either—she'd had no trouble getting the message. He looked down on her, judged her and found her not up to his oh-so-pure standards.

Well, whatever his private views, he'd sure come along at the right moment, for which she was profoundly grateful.

"Actually, I was just leaving," she told him before turning to face Ray. "I mean what I said, Ray. Don't pursue it. It's not going to happen."

"You threatening me, *chica?*"

Stepping into the room, the cop put himself between her and Ray. The lawman had at least five inches on her long-ago lover, and he used every one of them to intimidate the shorter man. "I don't believe she was threatening you, Mr...? Excuse me, I didn't catch your last name."

"None of your business."

The lawman's back was broad, his neck thick.

"Care to tell me Ray's last name, Ms. Garner?" He didn't shift around to face her—probably doing that staring thing with Ray that men seemed to find so compelling. "Has he been threatening you? Do you want to file charges?"

Jackson waited for the woman's answer, but he heard nothing from her. He angled his body slightly, just enough to see a look pass between her and Ray. For a brief moment they connected, leaving him out of the equation. Whatever silent messages they sent to each other, something had been decided.

Vanessa Garner looked up at him with a tight-lipped smile. "We were just having a little give and take," she said in that low, throaty voice of hers. "It's over now. Thanks, Detective. I'm sorry, I don't remember your name."

"It's Jackson Rutherford, ma'am. With the Pacific Community Police Department over on Culver, if you— if either of you," he amended pointedly, "ever needs to get hold of me."

She offered him another small, humorless smile, letting him know his lack of subtlety was appreciated.

She was shorter than he'd thought earlier, no more than five-four without the heels. And her eyes, under the single naked lightbulb, were the color of the Pacific Ocean on a sunny day, not dark, not pale, but richly, intensely blue-green. And just plain heart-stoppingly gorgeous.

"Thank you, Detective," she said solemnly. "I'll remember that. My aunt and my kids are waiting for me. I have to go now. Goodbye."

"I'll see you soon, *chica,*" the creep—whose last name he still didn't know—said.

"Not if I can help it," she retorted and walked out the door.

This was pretty amazing, Jackson thought, one of those being-in-the-right-place-at-the-right-time kind of things. And he was real glad he had been. As he'd been walking along after visiting the men's room, he'd heard angry voices behind the closed door. He'd overheard enough of the conversation to realize he'd been way off base about Vanessa Garner's reaction to Ray. The guy was *not* her dealer, she was *not* glad to see him.

But they did have a history, that he could tell—something to do with a beating—which wasn't a pleasant memory, at least not for her.

He watched her retreating form, thinking there was no way the skirt and jacket could mask the subtle sway of her hips, the long, shapely legs, the proud carriage. Ray was checking her out, too. Jackson turned his attention back to him, stared at him long and hard.

The shorter man glared back, defiant, not in the least afraid. "You like 'Nessa, huh?" he said with a knowing leer. "In the old days, I used to get good money for her services. You scoring some there, man? She sleeping with the pigs now?"

A sudden fierce rage boiled up inside him, and it took all his control not to backhand this little scumbag across the face. Instead, Jackson favored him with his coldest, steeliest glare. "I'll ignore that," he said softly. "One time only. But I want you to know that you do anything to her, I mean anything, and I'll make your life a living hell."

Ray raised an insolent eyebrow. "Oh, yeah? Watch me. I'm shaking with fear." With that, he spat on the floor, then sauntered past Jackson toward the door.

The detective grabbed his arm, spun him around. "I mean what I say, Ray."

"So do I, *cerdo.*" Jerking his arm away, he walked out.

Over the years Jackson had learned not to let taunts made by lowlifes get to him—it was just macho posturing and not worth his energy. But this little creep had gotten past his defenses. Maybe because there was a woman involved and his early training had taught him to protect and defend the weaker sex.

Or maybe—with a less honorable reading of the situation, he ruefully admitted—it was because he'd found himself attracted to the woman, even though he'd been careful to hide it, and Ray had seen right through him.

Frowning, Jackson followed Ray out to the parking lot, saw him get into his car, a black Mercedes sedan, and drive away. He took out his notebook and wrote down the license plate number for future reference.

The sound of children's laughter drew his attention back to the parking lot. Several yards away, he saw Vanessa surrounded by an older Latina woman and three kids. They'd been down front in the audience earlier. Good-looking kids. A cute little girl, two older boys in suits, all of them hugging her.

Her face radiant with joy, she looked up, met his gaze for a brief moment, then—the inner light of happiness gone from her expression—nodded solemnly at him. It was, he guessed, a kind of grudging thank-you.

He nodded back. Glad to be of service, ma'am, he thought silently, then watched as she headed off with her family. Watched her shiny black hair swishing between her shoulder blades, the easy sway of her skirt hem, those pretty, shapely calves and ankles…

He hissed in a breath. Damn, he thought, how low could a body get? He'd heard the woman's story today, knew that she'd been used and abused by men all her life. Yet here he was, ogling her, lusting after her, when she deserved much better than that.

Yeah, he'd been just plain wrong about Vanessa Garner, that was for sure. Now that he knew about her background, what she'd come from; now that he'd witnessed her facing down her ex-pimp—if what Ray had said was the truth—and seen her beaming with maternal joy when she was with her kids, yeah, he'd been plum wrong to lump her into the category of ex-junkies who weren't nearly as "ex" as they wanted the world to think them. He'd gotten a tad cynical in his years on the force, but he needed to reserve that cynicism for the dealers and corrupters of youth he saw every day, not for the truly heroic.

He continued to watch Vanessa Garner as she and her family stopped at an old Chevy sedan and began to pile in. No two ways about it, she was one interesting woman. She'd handled herself pretty well with the creep, but that particular story wasn't over yet. He wondered how far Ray would go and if she would seek some kind of police protection from him, or if she'd tough it out.

Yes, an interesting woman, one he might like to get to know better.

Except…

It probably would not be real smart to take up with Vanessa Garner. Admirable she might be, but she was still an ex-addict, an ex-hooker and the mother of three. If he were answering a personal ad, any one of those particulars would have crossed her off the list of potentials.

And then, of course, there was Mama's voice inside his head. More so lately, as she'd been making noises about coming out for a visit and he'd been putting her off. Mental note: deal with Mama, and soon.

A person of color? he could imagine her saying about Vanessa Garner. *I have nothing against a person of color, of course, nothing against them making their way in the world, getting an education, having a fine job, raising a fine colored family. Nothing wrong with it at all. But it's always best to keep the races separate, don't you agree? Less complications, less chance of problems developing down the road.*

Mama believed what she believed, no two ways about it. She was a throwback; she'd let the real world and its changes pass her by. Not Jackson. He'd traveled and studied. He lived in—hell, he *embraced* the real world.

Still, it seemed that, in the matter of Vanessa Garner, both his and his mama's worldviews were in agreement. The woman had way too much baggage, so he would not be pursuing her; there would be no "down the road" for the two of them. And if that thought brought a sudden, totally unexpected wave of disappointment with it, then that was simply the way it went sometimes.

His stomach growled. He glanced at his watch. Well, of course—no time for breakfast and nearly lunchtime. He would grab a burger before heading over to the station to catch up on paperwork. He'd done the community relations thing, bailed Sal out. His partner owed him.

And the mean streets of Los Angeles, California, awaited.

Chapter 2

"I love you, baby," Vanessa said, squatting to give Katy a quick hug.

"I'm not a baby."

"I know, but you're *my* baby. Be careful today."

Katy rolled her eyes upward, looking amazingly like her older brother, Thomas, at that moment. "I know, Mommy. 'Don't talk to strangers.' Can I go now?"

Here, inside the chain-link fence, the schoolyard was filled with children screaming and laughing and running around. The noise was deafening. Vanessa cupped her little girl's face and said, "And if one approaches you, run the other way and scream as loud as you can."

"Mommy," Katy said, squirming. "I'm going to be late."

"Tell me you understand."

"I do. I understand. Promise."

Vanessa searched her child's face for another long moment, then dropped her hands and stood up again. "Go. Have a good day."

She watched Katy, her little ball of energy and questions, run off, to be swallowed up immediately by a small crowd of other six-year-olds, laughing and skipping and just being children. Oh, God, she thought, feeling her heart clutch up. What can I do to protect her? How can I make her safe? Not just from Ray, but from life.

Deep in thought she headed back to her car. Her own childhood hadn't been anything close to safe, with Mom's drinking and a series of stepfathers. Sober, Mom had done her best, but as the years went on, she'd seldom been sober, so Vanessa had had to learn to take care of herself starting way too young. By the time her mother died, when Katy was a year old, Vanessa had ceased to think of her as any kind of parent at all.

Katy and the boys were having a different experience with her, that much she knew, for the past five years. She felt proud of herself for this fact, at least; she was drug free and present for them. They were what had gotten her through rehab and kept her going all day, every day. And she had thought they were all doing okay, that she'd managed to escape retribution for her past. Like a fool, she'd even begun to relax a little.

Until Ray showed up. Saturday had been the award presentation, and today was Tuesday. Three days since she'd had that run-in with him and no word from him yet. Katy's school seemed pretty safe, as was the child care afterward—even so, she'd let those in charge know that extra caution was needed for a while, and to be on the lookout for Katy's father, who had been in jail and did not have custody or any rights to her.

But no one was safe from Ray when he made up his mind. And Vanessa knew from previous experience that she couldn't predict what he would do, which was how he had kept his hold on her for four years. You could never tell when or from what direction the punishment would be coming, so you were always on guard and always scared.

She sighed, starting up the car and driving off to her job. When would he make his move? she wondered. Because he would, she had no doubt of it. Ray had decided he wanted his child and in his mind Vanessa was a pesky fly he needed to swat out of the way to get to his goal.

"Shane, take those earphones off right now."

"Music helps me study."

"Your teacher says different. Take them off."

Her fourteen-year-old gave her a look of disgust. "My teacher is lame."

Vanessa lifted the cover of the pot and took a sniff. The stew needed more garlic, maybe a little basil. "Put them away or I'll do it for you, Shane. I mean it."

"Told you," twelve-year-old Thomas said, followed shortly by, "Mom, he kicked me."

"Both of you, cut it out."

There was peace in the kitchen for a while after that, and she savored the moment. Something good on the stove, her three children at the table, the boys doing homework, Katy playing with her Barbie dolls. Vanessa had been up since 6:30 that morning, got the kids off to school, put in a full day's work, picked Katy up from day care and the boys from after-school activities. Now they would have dinner, then she would take off for her night class at Santa Monica City College. When she got home, she would study for an hour, turn in, get six hours sleep and start over.

So here in the small apartment kitchen, with its chipped tile and aging linoleum, the quiet—for however long it lasted—was precious to her.

It lasted about thirty seconds.

"I'm starving, "Thomas said.

"Ten more minutes."

"But I'm starving now," he whined.

"You had a sandwich an hour ago. Where do you put it?"

At that moment the wall phone rang. All three kids got up to answer it, scrambling and pushing at each other as they did.

Shane won. "'Sup?" he said with expectation on his face. Probably thinking it was from Lanetta, his sort-of girlfriend. But his expression quickly soured. "Yeah. Hold on." He handed the phone to his mother. "It's for you."

"Who is it?"

"Some guy."

She wiped her hands on a dish towel, then took the receiver. "Hello?"

There was silence for a moment. Then, "Ms. Garner?"

"Yes, who is this?"

"Jackson Rutherford."

"Who?"

"Detective Rutherford. We met the other day when you were getting that award?"

A picture formed in her mind then. Big and very broad. Southern. Strong. Scary. Also surprisingly protective, chivalrous even, something she hadn't come in contact with much in her life. If ever.

"Oh, yes. I remember you, Detective."

"How are you?"

"I'm fine."

She waited. What in the world did he want? Whatever it was, he didn't seem anxious to spit it out, because there were some more beats of silence. Oh, no, maybe there was bad news. "Is anything wrong?"

"No. No, not at all. I just wondered…"

Again, he paused. So she prompted. "Yes?"

"If that man who was hassling you has been any problem?"

The rest of the picture formed now, and it all came back to her: the scene in the storeroom, the feelings of terror. Ray and his threats. As the week had gone on, and there'd been nothing more from Ray, she'd managed to put all that on the back burner. Now it was front and center.

Which didn't make her at all pleased with this cop for reminding her. "No, I haven't heard from him," she said.

"I looked him up. Romeo Ortiz." The Southern drawl was particularly strong as he pronounced Ray's name. "He has a record."

"Yes, I know that."

"So, I was just. Well…"

On the other end of the line, Jackson winced then looked up at the ceiling for inspiration. He was thoroughly disgusted with himself. What was up with this? What was the matter with him? He was all squirrelly, like he was seventeen years old and trying to get up the nerve to ask a girl to the prom but unable to spit it out.

"Well what?" He heard the impatience in her voice—hell, who could blame her?

"See," he tried, "the thing is…"

He was pretty okay with words, knew how to string them together so they made sense, could usually say what needed saying. But now that his opening line had been delivered, he couldn't seem to wrap his mouth around the real reason he'd called. *I've been thinking about you since Saturday. Can't get you out of my mind, actually, even though there is no way we could have any kind of future together. Still, I want to see you, to be with you. What's your thinking on that?*

Simple, but not appropriate. So he said nothing. Again.

Vanessa Garner let out an impatient sigh. "Look, Detective, I have to go. I have something on the stove."

"Oh. You're cooking dinner?"

"It *is* dinnertime, so, yes."

Sarcasm, he thought. Okay, he could deal with sarcasm. But she was about to hang up, he could sense it. He couldn't let her, so he just plum blurted it out. "Would you like to have a cup of coffee…or something…sometime?"

He squeezed his eyes shut. *Lame. Stupid.*

But, hell, at least it was out there now, and he waited for her response. However, now it was Vanessa Garner's turn to be silent. He held his breath. Had he ever sounded more like a witless fool in his life?

He glanced quickly around the squad room one more time, to make sure no one was witnessing his piss-poor attempt to ask a woman out. And, whew, no one was anywhere nearby. His partner, Sal, was still using his vacation time to be with his wife and newborn, so the nearby desk was empty. Others were way over by the coffee machine, laughing over some perp and his bizarre rationalizations for being caught with valuable diamonds up his nose.

Finally she spoke. "You mean, like on a date?" That throaty, sexy voice of hers asked this quietly, as though she were trying not to be overheard.

"No," was the quick answer, but just as quickly, he said, "Or yes. Well, sort of. You know. Coffee. Nothing fancy."

After what seemed like an eternity, she said, "I'm flattered. Thank you. But I don't really have time."

"Well now, that seems a shame. Why not?"

"I have three kids, a full-time job, and I go to school. Not a lot of minutes left in my day."

"What do you do for relaxation?"

"Look, I really don't have time."

He smiled, leaned back in his desk chair, propped his size thirteens on the desk, settling in for a little chat. He felt much less nervous now. "See? That's what I mean. A body needs some down time, so we have to find a way to get you some."

"I meant I don't have time to talk to you at this moment."

"Oh. Well then, how about I call b—"

"I really have to go now," she interrupted quickly. "Thanks for…asking." And with that she hung up.

Jackson stared at the phone, his brow furrowed.

After all he'd been through this week, going back and forth about contacting her, trying to talk himself out of it because, face it, this was not a good idea. But then finally deciding what the hell, making the move, and… nothing.

He'd been given the brush-off. Totally and thoroughly rejected.

Which, truth be told, threw him. He wasn't used to being turned down. Not that he was any big-time player, but, hell, he'd had his share of women, and when he liked one, it was usually mutual.

Not this time. It seemed Vanessa Garner was immune to his charms. He frowned, not at all pleased.

But hey, he told himself, he would live.

Vanessa looked up from the paperwork on her desk and gazed out the window of her office. Her view was the employee parking lot and, past that, rows of yellow vans and busses, transportation for kids at private schools all over Los Angeles. It was a good business, a thriving business, and not for the first time, she felt enormous gratitude that she worked here. She'd started at the bottom, as a receptionist, right out of rehab—the owner's son had died of an overdose, and the older man, Clarence Todd, had become active in drug prevention programs. A Single Voice had gotten her the interview and Mr. Todd had given her a chance. After that, she'd worked her butt off to show all of them that their faith in her had been justified.

From receptionist she'd gone to scheduler, and from there, assistant manager, till her most recent promotion, manager. She had eight employees in the office and a fleet of thirty busses and their drivers to manage. She was constantly busy, putting out fires, dealing with complaints and illnesses, supervising new office staff and working out systems to streamline everything. The phone was constant.

The intercom buzzer brought her out of her reverie. It was Renee, the new receptionist. "Call for you."

"What line?"

"Oh, yeah. Two."

"Who is it?"

"He didn't say." She sounded bored.

"Renee, you're supposed to ask their name and the nature of their business, remember?"

"Oh, yeah, right." Vanessa heard the sound of cracking gum and shook her head. Hired on Monday, Renee had had two days to learn the ropes. Learn them? She hadn't even begun to climb them. She wouldn't last long. "Okay, wait a second and I'll find out."

"Never mind." She pressed the button for line two and put it on speakerphone. "This is Vanessa Garner."

"Hey, *chica.*"

Instant chill flooded her veins. She hadn't seen or heard from Ray in a week and a half. Had she begun to think he would just go away? If she had, she was a fool.

She picked up the receiver. "Yes, Ray?" she said coolly.

"How's it going?"

She cut right to the chase. "Why are you calling?"

"I been out of town and I wondered if you'd changed your mind. About the kid."

"Her name is Katy and you know how I feel about it. The answer is no."

She heard him taking in a quick breath, trying to control his temper. "I'm asking nice, 'Nessa."

She remembered that temper, remembered the damage it could do. But he mustn't sense her fear—that was what he thrived on. "I appreciate you asking nice, Ray. But it's still no."

"Man, you don't get it. Sharon, she's all the time crying because she can't have any babies. It's a real drag, you know?"

What was up with this man? He wanted Vanessa to feel sorry for his wife? To make it better by handing over her child? What planet did he live on?

"So adopt."

"Some other guy's kid? No way."

She took a quick moment to tamp down her irritation. "Ray. Please. I'm sorry for your wife, but Katy's mine. I really don't have anything else to say to you." With that, she hung up.

She stared at the phone, tried not to panic. What would be Ray's next move? Whatever it was, it wouldn't be pretty. And what could she, should she, do about it?

She gazed at the framed picture on her desk, the one of the four of them that Aunt Lupe had taken last year. Three beautiful children—even Shane had managed a smile—were gathered around her. Her smile was the broadest. And why not? She'd worked like crazy to get all of them under the same roof, to cook them good meals and watch them do their homework. She'd gone through way too much pain and heartache.

And now Ray was back and all of it could topple over, just like that.

Maybe they should move—she could change her name, change all the kids' names. It might be the only answer, because when Ray wanted something he was like a shark moving through the deep waters of the ocean, mouth open, devouring everything that came in his path.

Again, she gazed out the window. Her day had begun so nicely, a typical spring day in early May. But even though the Southern California skies were predictably sunny, a cloud cover swept over her mood. And the small chill of fear lodged itself in her heart.

It wasn't often that Jackson got a chance to do his ten-mile run in the late afternoon, but his hours had changed this week; on Wednesdays he was in earlier and out earlier. So instead of the sun just coming up as he approached Pacific Avenue, it was headed the other direction, on its way to disappearing behind the Pacific Ocean. He'd worked up a healthy sweat—should he change before popping in on Mac? But the fact that he was so near his destination decided him. It would take too much time to go home and then come back. He and Mac, whose actual name was Macklin Thurgood Marshall, Jr., didn't stand on ceremony, anyway.

When Jackson got to the correct address, he stopped and gazed at a two-story building, the lower level consisting of a shabby storefront built of old, dirty brick surrounding a wide display window. Across the glass there was lettering but the glare from the late-afternoon sun made it difficult to read. He moved in closer until he made out The Last House on the Block. Underneath in smaller letters, it said Legal and Other Help. Pay What You Can.

He pushed open the door and walked in to find himself in a room about fifteen by twenty. Mac was in the far corner, seated at an old desk and looking through some papers, reading glasses perched on his nose.

"May I help you?" The sound, a lilting, faintly Hispanic one, came from the left. He turned to see a middle-aged woman seated behind another desk, equally used looking. She had a broad Indian face and a silver-streaked black bun perched on the top of her head. A gold cross hung from a chain around her neck. Her smile was welcoming, and she looked familiar— had he met her?

Before he could respond, Mac was out of his chair and walking toward him, hand extended, a smile creasing his lined brown face. "Jackson, my man," he said in that deep bass voice of his. "Good to see you."

Jackson swiped his palm across his sweatshirt, then shook his friend's hand. He hadn't seen Mac in months, and it seemed to him that the older man's hair was even grayer now. He wore much-washed baggy chinos and a faded plaid shirt. "Yeah, you too, Mac. I called Wanda and she said you were spending all your time here. What happened to retirement?"

He shrugged. "Tried fishing, tried to find a hobby, nothing worked. I like it here." He gestured with his hand. "You get another view of humanity, different from the one we got on the job." He stood back, looked his ex-partner up and down. "You're as dis-gustingly fit as ever."

It was Jackson's turn to shrug. "I do my bit."

"Never did get into exercising." Mac clapped him on

the shoulder, then indicated the other desk in the room. "This here's our receptionist, Guadalupe Delgado. Lupe, meet my former partner, Jackson Rutherford."

Jackson turned again to the middle-aged Latina, then snapped his fingers. "You were with Ms. Garner weekend before last, at that awards thing."

"And you were on the dais." She nodded. "Yes, I'm her aunt."

Interesting. Small world for sure. "Well, tell her I said hello, okay?"

"I'll be glad to."

Mac said, "So, this a social call or what?"

Jackson gazed around, looking for somewhere private so they could talk. Apart from the two desks, there was a small love seat, two chairs, a couple of plants and some pictures on the walls. The far-left corner contained a box with children's toys and a small slide. There were two doors on the far wall, one marked Rest Room. He pointed to the other. "Where does that lead?"

"To Shannon Coyle's office. She's the founder of the place, a lawyer. Twisted my arm to come here. She can be very persuasive."

"Right. She was at that thing for Ms. Garner, too. Feel like getting a beer? Or rather, feel like watching me get a beer?" he said, remembering that Mac didn't drink.

"Can't think of a thing I'd like better."

They went to a neighborhood bar down the street. It was cool inside, dimly lit, filled mostly with men. There was a pool game going on in the rear, a TV set was tuned soundlessly to a baseball game, and over the loudspeakers came Joe Cocker singing "You Are So Beautiful." They sat on stools and Jackson ordered a cold one. Mac got a tonic with a twist.

"You're still doing great," Jackson observed, "I mean, with the drinking."

"Eight years clean and sober."

"Yeah, you had quit just before I transferred here."

Mac chuckled. "You put up with a lot of crap from me in the beginning. For a while there, a long while, I was not a pleasant person to be around."

"Hey, you put up with me, too, remember?"

"You still had too much Marine in you. Not to mention way too much good ol' boy."

Jackson's mouth quirked upward. "You knocked both of 'em out of me pretty quick."

"One of my proudest accomplishments. You've turned out just fine." They grinned at each other, clicked glasses and drank. Then Mac raised an inquiring eyebrow. "So what's up?"

Not sure if he'd done the right thing by coming to Mac, Jackson rubbed a hand over the top of his head. "I need a little advice."

"I'm your man."

"It's about a girl."

"Oh. Well then, I might not be your man. Been with one woman for thirty years."

"But you know about women. They always like you, trust you on sight."

Mac shot him a knowing look. "From what I've seen you're pretty intimate with the fair sex yourself."

"No, I mean…" He stopped. Back to feeling like a

seventeen-year-old again. And he was twice that age plus four more. He shook his head.

"Son," Mac said. "Just what *do* you mean? Spit it out."

He took a slug of his beer, set his glass down. "There's this woman. Lupe's niece, actually."

"Vanessa?"

"You know her?"

"Well, sure. She and the kids come over to the storefront sometimes. Beautiful woman. She's had a tough life."

Jackson nodded. "Yeah, I know. Heard the whole thing. Street, drugs, rehab. All of it. Remember? I was at that ceremony for her couple of weeks back. Why weren't you there, by the way?"

"I was down with bronchitis, had to miss it. So you like her."

"Well…" He shrugged. "Yeah."

Mac met his gaze, looked at him long and hard. "What exactly are you asking me?"

"I called her. A week ago. Asked her out for coffee. She turned me down cold, said she didn't have time. Job, school, three kids."

"Sounds like she was telling the truth."

"Yeah, but the thing is, Mac," he said, annoyed with himself all over again, "I can't get the damn woman out of my head."

The Stones' "Ruby Tuesday" was up next on the speakers and Jackson had a brief high school memory of necking in the back of a pickup while the radio was tuned to an oldies station. It had been one hot and heavy night, for sure.

"And, by the way," he told Mac, "in case you're feeling all protective about her, it's more than sex."

"Okay."

"Or not," he added, in the interest of full disclosure. "Hell, I don't know. I mean, how am I supposed to know? She turned me down."

"Wow," Mac said softly. "I've never seen you like this, Jackson. She really got to you." At Jackson's embarrassed shrug, he asked, "So what's the real reason she turned you down, do you think?"

"Could be what she said. Or maybe she just plain isn't interested."

"But you're not ready to give up." It wasn't a question.

"Wouldn't like myself if I didn't give it another try. Besides, Mac, like I said, I can't get the damn woman out of my head. She's buzzing around in there like a June bug on a string."

As Mac pondered his friend, a smug, superior smile formed on his face. "Got it bad, son, huh?"

"Yeah, yeah, yeah. Don't make me sorry I told you this."

Thoughtfully, Mac took a drink, then chewed on the lime for a bit before setting it down on the napkin. "You know what Wanda would say?"

"What?"

"Send her flowers."

"You serious?"

"Couldn't be more so."

He frowned, considered it. "Flowers, huh? Doesn't that make it too big a deal?"

"Lets her know you're interested, for sure."

"But doesn't that seem, well, *too* interested? Like some kind of…declaration or something? I mean, hell, I barely know the woman."

"And if you do nothing, you will remain barely knowing her."

He thought it over, nodded. Not that he was pleased, but he could see the logic. In for a penny, in for a pound. "I guess."

Now Mac's grin was huge, all white teeth and dancing brown eyes. "I mean it, I have never seen you like this, Jackson."

"Just don't make a big fuss about it, okay?"

"Right."

"And don't tell anyone down at the precinct, you know, if you happen to see any of them."

"My lips are sealed."

He downed the last of his beer, then scowled at Mac. "And stop looking at me like you're my father and I'm some poor lovesick slob. I barely know the woman."

"So you said."

Jackson threw down some bills and rose from his stool. "Come on, *Dad,* let's get out of here."

"Glad to, *Son.*"

Mac's laughter followed him out the door and onto the street.

Vanessa glanced away from the computer screen and at her watch. 5:00 p.m. Usually about this time, Lupe would be picking up the kids for their traditional Thursday night dinner together. It gave her aunt some time alone with the children she'd helped raise and

Vanessa a much-needed three hours to herself. But tonight Lupe had had to cancel—some kind of staff meeting at The Last House on the Block. Which meant Vanessa had to leave now to get the kids.

Her intercom buzzed. "There's a man here to see you," Renee said.

She felt a now-familiar chill at the news; Ray had called at about the same time yesterday. Was he here to harass her in person? "Who is it?"

"A Mr. Constantine."

"I don't know any Mr. Constantine."

"He's says he's a lawyer, Vanessa. Shall I send him back?"

She felt herself relax slightly. There were a couple of nuisance lawsuits the company was dealing with at the moment. It was probably one of those. What she ought to do was ask Renee to inform the visitor that he needed to set up an appointment. But perhaps it was something Vanessa might be able to handle quickly herself. "No, I'm just leaving. I'll meet him up front."

The lawyer was medium height and olive skinned, with dyed black hair cut expensively and a gorgeous charcoal-gray suit that nearly masked a middle-aged pot belly. She mistrusted him on sight.

He offered his hand. "Ms. Garner?"

She shook it briefly. "Mr. Constantine. What can I do for you?"

He handed her a card. She glanced at it. Full name, Philip M. Constantine. Offices in Beverly Hills. The high-status section between Wilshire and Santa Monica Boulevards.

"May we talk privately?" he said.

"I can give you a couple of minutes. I'm on my way home."

"Then why don't I walk you to your car."

She glanced out the window. It was still daylight, others were milling around the parking lot. She would be fine. She nodded. "Good night, Renee," she said, still on the fence about the girl and her possibilities. She'd seen a glimmer of intelligence as the week had gone on. Perhaps she could learn, perhaps Vanessa could have some patience and work with the girl, give her a chance, the way others had given her a chance.

She pushed open the glass door and walked through, Constantine right behind her.

"I represent Romeo Ortiz."

For some reason she wasn't really surprised. "All right."

"Mr. Ortiz would like to meet with you."

She walked quickly; the man had short legs and had to scurry to keep up with her. "Not interested."

"I think you'll want to hear what Mr. Ortiz has to say."

"Still not interested."

With surprising quickness, he got in front of her, planted himself so she had to stop and look at him. She could see from his expression that he wasn't pleased by her attitude.

"Look, Ms. Garner, we can do this nicely or I can start with subpoenas and lawsuits and I promise the paperwork will keep you occupied for weeks. Or you can just do this one thing. Come to my office tomorrow night. Is six convenient for you? Bring your lawyer. I'm sure we can work this out amicably."

"There *is* no way to work this out, Mr. Constantine, amicably or otherwise."

"Come to my office," he repeated, as though he had not a doubt she would do so. "We'll see."

He walked away, leaving her standing in the middle of the parking lot looking after him. A heavy load of depression descended on her as she made her way to her car. Ray. Back and refusing to leave. Sending his lawyer now. After that, who knew? She really might have to move.

She picked up Katy from day care, and got to listen to her little girl chattering happily about the book her teacher had read to them and how she was getting to know the alphabet and how Matthew Chin still wet his pants sometimes and how Brenda McMasters said a bad word and had to go to the principal's office. At the end of the school year, she and her class would sing in a show and Katy would get to wear a flower costume.

By the time they walked into the apartment and were greeted with the smell of roasting chicken, Vanessa was smiling. Shane had remembered to put the casserole in the oven for once.

Before she got the door closed behind her, Thomas ran up to her and pointed to the kitchen table. "Mom, look!"

In the middle of the old wooden table stood a bouquet of flowers in a glass vase. Lots of flowers, a mixture of lilies and carnations and daisies, a riot of color. She stared. It wasn't her birthday. Who would send her flowers?

In an instant her up mood plummeted. Ray? Trying to soften her up? What, did he think she was stupid?

She frowned at Thomas. "When did these come? Did you let the delivery boy in?"

"No, Mom," he said, rolling his eyes heavenward at how much his mom didn't get that he knew what to do. "We didn't let anyone in. Mrs. Contreras next door, she kept them for us, gave them to us when Shane and me got home."

"Shane and I," she corrected automatically.

"Whatever. Look there's a card. Open it, okay?"

She didn't want to. If it was from Ray—and she really couldn't think of anyone else who would send flowers—then she would toss the blooms in the garbage.

Still, she knew she had to find out. She plucked the card from the plastic holder and opened it. Inside, there was no message, just a name.

Jackson Rutherford.

Her eyes widened with surprise. The cop. She'd been sent flowers by the cop.

She was being courted by a cop.

It was ludicrous. Too much.

And yet, she couldn't help a small smile of pleasure. Vanessa was thirty years old, and for the first time in her life a man had sent her flowers.

Chapter 3

"Thanks so much for picking me up, Shannon," Vanessa said on Friday night, adjusting her seat belt. "And for doing this. Hey, thanks for all of it," she added with grateful smile. "I'm semiterrified."

"Are you kidding?" Shannon Coyle checked her mirrors before pulling out into traffic. "This is what I do, represent the little guy in front of the big guys. Especially when the big guy is Phil Constantine, number-one sleaze." She grinned happily. "Can't wait."

"One of these days I'm going to pay you back for all you've done."

Shannon, short and round, with a mop of dark, curly hair, and who was a few years older than Vanessa, darted her a look before returning her attention to the road. "You know what? I'm tired of that one. The Last House on the Block is there to work pro bono for those who need it. You need it. You pay me back by doing what you're doing—getting on with your life." She chuckled. "Besides, your aunt Lupe would murder me if I ever took any money from you, not to mention quit her job, and the place couldn't run without Lupe."

Vanessa had no answer to this. She never did. Shannon had acted as her lawyer a couple of other times and had always refused payment of any sort. "It feels like charity."

"Charity is given when someone is unable to do for themselves. You do plenty, so get over yourself. And I'm changing the subject to our upcoming meeting. Tell me about Ray Ortiz."

Not Vanessa's favorite topic, for sure. She sighed. "You already know the basics—I met him when I was nineteen, when Shane was three and Thomas one. He was my connection first, then my boyfriend and then my pimp."

She might not have spoken of her history in this matter-of-fact way with others, but Shannon had become a close friend over the past couple of years since Aunt Lupe had introduced them. In fact, Shannon was one of her first female friends and had never, not once, seemed to pass judgment on her.

"I couldn't get away from him, although I tried several times, but he always brought me back. That's the thing with dope—it takes away your will, not to mention your mind."

"I know he beat you when you were pregnant with Katy. Was that the first time?"

"Hardly. The thing was I hated hooking, just *hated* it.

The only way I could get through it was go far away in my head, and that took a lot of crack. Ray used to rough me up regularly for not being good at my job." Frowning, she shook her head. "It's amazing when I think about that time. It's not only a whole other life but sometimes it feels like it happened to a whole other person."

Shannon shot her an I-hear-you smile. "You *were* a whole other person. So, back to Ray. How can you be sure Katy is his?"

"Because I wasn't with anyone else in that time period. His last beating broke my arm and I was in a cast for a couple of months and had to stay home."

"What a sweetheart," Shannon said with a disgusted shake of her head.

"The saddest part is that I thought I deserved it, Shannon. It was about my lowest point. The beginning of the end of Vanessa the First."

They didn't talk for a while as Shannon maneuvered the car through late-afternoon L.A. traffic, heading north from Venice, with its mix of up-and-comers, elderly pensioners, immigrants and gangbangers, toward the well-manicured streets of Beverly Hills, where only the wealthy need apply. Vanessa came here once in a great while to window-shop, just to sniff the air of everything that was out of her reach, and to remind herself that they were just *things*. She would tell herself that, in her children and in her struggle to become educated and have meaningful work, she had everything that was truly precious in life. Sometimes it worked; sometimes it left her yearning for just a little bit more.

A few blocks away from their destination, Shannon

said, "Fill me in on Ray's personality. I want to know what we're dealing with."

She thought about it for a moment, then said grimly, "He can be charming but he's ruthless. Has no conscience. He's single-minded. One time he beat up an old wino who used to sleep on the corner bus stop bench because Ray decided homeless people were an eyesore. No one stopped him—the whole block was terrified of him."

"Sounds like a sociopath."

"I guess he is." She smiled. "Now that I know what that word means."

Shannon gave her an answering grin. "Ain't education great?"

"The greatest."

After parking, Shannon glanced at her watch. "There's enough time. Good. We're meeting someone at Starbucks."

As they walked into the coffee place, a man seated at a table rose and made his way toward them. Vanessa stopped in her tracks and stared. It was that cop, Jackson Rutherford. He was out of uniform, dressed in jeans and a short-sleeved black T-shirt. None of his clothing was tight enough to be called body hugging, but there was no way to miss the well-developed biceps and broad chest, the long, muscular, denim-clad legs. He could be a walking advertisement for a body-building gym.

Vanessa put her hand on Shannon's arm. "Is this who we're supposed to meet?"

"Jackson? Yeah. He's a friend of Mac Marshall's, you know, the ex-cop who's on staff? Jackson offered to come with us tonight."

By then, the big detective was standing in front of them, and Vanessa looked up and met his gaze. She hitched in a surprised breath, startled by how downright imposing he was, all hard muscle and brawn. He towered over her, even with her in heels. He wasn't wearing his sunglasses tonight, and she could see that his face was all hard angles and planes. A long, slightly crooked nose, razor sharp cheekbones and dark-brown stubble covering a strong jawline.

And beneath fierce brown eyebrows, the most startling blue eyes. Really amazing blue eyes, she couldn't help observing, not cold and hard, which a lot of blue eyes could be, but vibrant, filled with life.

This man, all power and confidence—pure manliness—didn't match up with the tentative voice on the phone a few days before, nor someone who would send her flowers. Who was he, really?

He nodded politely at both women. "Ms. Coyle, Ms. Garner."

"Shannon and Vanessa, Detective," the lawyer said with a grin. "This is L.A. We do first names only on the West Coast, remember?"

One side of his mouth quirked up, and his blue eyes lit with humor. "Then please call me Jackson." Vanessa hadn't seen anything resembling warmth or humor in their single previous meeting, when he'd been all threats and head butting with Ray, and again it threw her.

"Why are you here?" she blurted out, but before he answered, turned to Shannon. "Why is he here?"

"Muscle. Shall we sit?"

As they walked over to a table, Jackson said in that

faint Southern drawl of his, "May I get you ladies some coffee?"

"Largest they got. Black," Shannon said, sitting. "Vanessa?"

She was dying for a cup of something hot and tasty, not to mention a shot of caffeine for courage. She fumbled in her purse for some change. "A grande latte with skim milk."

"Put your money away," he said, then took off before she had time to protest.

Vanessa watched him leave, then turned again to Shannon who had also been staring. "Muscle? What's that about?"

Instead of answering, Shannon grinned at the sight of Jackson's back, which was as impressive as Jackson's front. "Isn't he just a beautiful example of the species?"

"What species?"

"Manly men." She made a growling sound in the back of her throat. "Gotta love 'em."

"Is he a…particular friend of yours?" She said it conversationally, but was surprised at how much she wanted the answer to be either "No" or "Just friends, nothing more."

Shannon shook her head. "After you called yesterday about this meeting tonight, I asked Mac if he knew any threatening-looking guys and he suggested Jackson. When I called him, he reminded me that we'd met at that award thing in your honor."

"But he's a cop. Won't he get in trouble if he tries to strong-arm anyone?"

"He says he's off duty and won't do a thing except look mean if necessary. Nothing hands-on." Shannon shrugged, grinned again. "Hey, if he says he's cool with it, who am I to protest?"

"Okay, but again, why do we need muscle? I thought this was just a conference."

"Phil Constantine is scum of the worst kind. All his clients are even bigger scumbags. He defends drug dealers, rapists, stalkers, mob guys. Which means we need to play hardball with him. Jackson is our version of hardball. If this Ray Ortiz pulls anything physical, if he has one of his goons with him, we have our own goon. It shows we know the score."

Jackson returned with the coffee. As he set Vanessa's down in front of her, their eyes met briefly, and in that moment she saw a look in his that took her breath away. A mixture of heat and hesitation, with an overlay of irritation, as though he was not sure of himself and not real happy to be feeling this way. It was disquieting to see in those astonishing eyes that hint of vulnerability. It revealed so much about a man who, in person at least, seemed nothing more than muscle and in-your-face toughness.

And it caused a little tug at something inside her, at a wall that she'd built around her heart many years before.

She averted her gaze, took a sip of her coffee.

She didn't like anyone getting through her barriers. Besides, she had no room for that kind of thing in her life. Even as that thought crossed her mind, another took its place: the flowers. The polite thing to do was to thank him for them. But not now, not in front of Shannon, for sure.

And maybe not at all. Better to just ignore the whole thing. Keep that barrier firmly in place.

Shannon looked from Vanessa to Jackson, then said, "Okay, here's the plan…"

With Jackson stationed in the waiting room, Vanessa and Shannon were shown into an empty conference room furnished with a long, antique table and upholstered side chairs. There was something comforting, Vanessa realized, about having two defenders with her today, one by her side and one close by, should he be needed. She'd had few if any defenders in her life; mostly she'd had to get through the difficult moments, not to mention years, on her own. And although she acknowledged the sense of comfort, it was also a little bit strange. She wasn't used to being taken care of, even temporarily, as this was.

The moment she and Shannon were seated, an inner door opened and Constantine and Ray came in and sat directly across from them. She made herself sit up straight, forced herself to meet Ray's gaze. What she found in his didn't surprise her—it was his cold, hard stare, the one that used to intimidate the hell out of her. He was trying to get her skin to crawl with dread, but she refused to let him get to her.

"Mr. Constantine?" Shannon said the moment they were all in position.

"Philip, please."

"Philip, fine. Why are we here?"

He splayed his hands; a diamond pinky ring sparkled in the overhead light. "It's a pretty simple matter, really. My client, Romeo Ortiz, admits paternity of Katherine Garner. I'm assuming there's no question of this?"

Shannon looked at Vanessa, who shook her head. "Ms. Garner agrees that the father of the last child she bore is Romeo Ortiz."

"I'm pleased we're not going to have any problems with paternity. In that case, my client would like to say something. Mr. Ortiz?"

Ray gave Vanessa a tight-lipped smile, even though his eyes didn't reflect any kind of joy in the least. "Here's the deal, *chica.*"

"Excuse me?" Shannon interrupted. "What did you call my client?"

"*Chica.* It's our little nickname."

"Her name is Vanessa Garner, *Ms.* Garner, and I'd appreciate you directing whatever you have to say to me."

Ray didn't like that, not in the least. Scowling, he darted a glance at Constantine, who nodded. Vanessa could see him controlling his temper as he turned back to stare at Shannon, a look of intense malevolence on his features for a brief moment before he relaxed his facial muscles and shrugged.

Then he smiled, went for the charming-Ray look. "All right, lawyer lady, here's the deal. Half a million."

Shannon didn't miss a beat. "The name is Ms. Coyle and half a million what?"

"Bucks. Smackers. Dollars. That's what I'll give her."

Constantine leaned in, adding smoothly, "What my client is saying is that he is willing to pay five hundred thousand dollars to Ms. Garner for the right to raise his own child. It's a very generous offer, as I'm sure you'll agree."

There was silence in the room for a few moments before Shannon cocked her head and said softly, "Counselor, surely you're not suggesting that Mr. Ortiz is trying to *buy* a six-year-old little girl?"

Constantine's smile was self-confident. "Not in the least. How can he buy what is already half-his? This is just a good-faith gift. He appreciates the years Ms. Garner has devoted to little Katy, the time and expense, and he feels compensation is the least he can do."

"And for that half a million, he wants what exactly? Spell it out for me."

"I want my kid," Ray said, meeting Vanessa's gaze with a look that said he meant business.

His lawyer put a hand on his arm. "Let me, Ray. Mr. Ortiz feels he has been deprived of watching his child grow up and would like to take her into his home and raise her. He feels—"

"Over my dead body."

It was out of her mouth before she could retrieve it.

She'd been good so far. Shannon had asked her not to speak unless she directed her to do so, and she'd done her best. But no way, no way in hell, would Ray Ortiz get his hands on her Katy.

She continued to lock eyes with him and saw in his all the cruelty he was capable of, the pain he could inflict if he chose to, but she just didn't care. "Let me repeat that," she said slowly and carefully, her own rage boiling hard just below the surface. "Not for half a million, not for a million. Not for any amount. Ever."

At the end of her pronouncement, there was again silence in the room. Then Constantine shuffled papers, sighed. "I had hoped we might do this quickly and smoothly, but it seems that we'll have to file papers for custody."

"Which will never be granted," Shannon said briskly. "Mr. Ortiz is a known drug dealer, a felon who has served time and who assaulted and nearly killed my client weeks before the child, *his* child, was born."

"She never filed charges."

"We have witnesses if it ever comes up. Signed affidavits. No judge in the world will award your client anything."

"And your client is a former addict and prostitute."

Shannon waved it away. "Years in the past. Don't even go there. She is a model citizen and mother. She has reformed, been honored by the community for it. Your client is still right in the thick of the drug trade."

"Prove it."

"We will if pushed, but trust me, you don't have a chance."

"We can tie you up in court for years. Mr. Ortiz is a successful businessman and has deep pockets."

"Fine," Shannon said. "I'm ready to take you and your client on. In the meantime, the child stays with her mother. And that is the end of the discussion." She rose, and so did Vanessa, deeply grateful she had this fierce lioness on her side.

Ray muttered a curse, but again Constantine put a steadying hand on his arm. "My client is willing to discuss joint custody."

"Not an option." The two women headed for the door.

"Surely he ought to have visitation rights," Constantine said.

Shannon stopped, turned around. "He's not trustworthy enough to bring her back when the visit's over. Sorry."

"What about supervised visitation?"

"What the hell is that?" Ray said.

Constantine explained, "You can be with your child, but someone appointed by the court would have to be with you at all times."

"No way," he said, a look of utter disbelief on his face.

"I guess we're done here," Shannon interrupted, then smiled at Vanessa. "Shall we?"

When the office door opened and Jackson saw the two women come through it, he stood quickly, searching both their faces for signs of how it had gone. Not real well, he thought. Shannon's expression was grim and so was Vanessa's, her hands fisted at her sides.

"You all right, ladies?"

Vanessa met his gaze, her own blazing with anger. "He wanted to buy my child," she said, her voice shaking with rage. "He offered me half a million dollars for my child."

"The man is a fool," he said softly.

"No, he's not a fool," Shannon offered. "He just hasn't come across anyone who can't be bought."

Vanessa shook her head. "Offering me money for my child, my baby, like she was a dress or a car."

"How did you leave it?" he asked.

Shannon's smile was mirthless. "With Mr. Ortiz sputtering."

At that moment, the object of their discussion yanked open the door to his lawyer's office and stormed into the anteroom, stopping short when he saw Vanessa. Pointing a finger at her, he said, "I tried this the legal way, *chica,* but after this, all bets are off."

"Hold it right there," Shannon said, about to move in, but Jackson, who had stood off to the side, held her arm, then inserted himself between Ray and Vanessa. Déjà vu all over again, he thought.

He met the dealer's hard gaze with a stone-cold one of his own. "Don't tell me you're threatening her again."

Ray frowned as he looked up at the huge policeman. "What are you doing here?"

"Friend of the family."

Ray stepped in closer, trying to take him on. "Yeah?"

Jackson stayed where he was, his eyes narrowed to slits. "Yeah."

He could see Ray wrestling with his temper, trying to decide just how much to push a cop. It took a lot of effort for the smaller man to rein it in, but he managed. With a disgusted exhalation, he whirled around and headed for the door. Before he left, his gaze roamed the room, making eye contact with Shannon, Vanessa and Jackson, one at a time. There was no mistaking the fury in his eyes. The man was deadly, no doubt about it.

After he walked out, slamming the door behind him, Shannon said, "Not a happy camper."

"He's trouble," Jackson offered. "Big-time trouble. If you want my opinion—"

The sound of a ringing cell phone pierced the

anteroom. Shannon reached into her purse and withdrew her phone then flipped it open.

"Shannon Coyle." She listened, frowned, then nodded. "I'll meet you at the West Hollywood station as soon as I can get there." She flipped the phone closed, put it back in her purse, then turned to Vanessa. "Got an emergency. Ex-husband nearly killed a client. Come on, I'll run you home first."

"West Hollywood is in the opposite direction. It's all right. I can take the bus."

"I'll drive you," Jackson said.

"Oh. I really couldn't—"

"You're a doll, Jackson," Shannon said with a grateful smile, "just like Mac said. Bless you. Vanessa, we'll talk tomorrow, okay?" And with that she was out the door of the office.

Vanessa had a look on her face that said she was not pleased to have her transportation issues settled by others. "Look, you really don't have to drive me."

"Sure I do," he said easily. "Ray could be waiting for you."

The stubborn expression on her face changed to one of utter seriousness as her eyes widened. "Of course. I hadn't thought of that."

"Come on."

He took her elbow and escorted her out the door and into the elevator. They rode down in silence. He picked up a whiff of—what? Lemons?—from her hair? Once outside the building, he looked both ways and in every shadowed corner before stepping onto the sidewalk. It was evening by now, and Beverly Hills was lit by soft streetlights and the headlights of passing high-priced sedans, convertibles and Hummers.

"Where are you parked?" she asked him.

"Around the corner."

They passed glittering stores, their windows filled with haute couture, designer clothing and accessories, jewelry, toys for children and grown-ups, scarves that cost a week's salary for most.

"You like walking around Beverly Hills?" he asked her.

"Occasionally. It's not real, somehow."

"Yeah, I know what you mean. All this wealth, in one place. A square mile or so of everything money can buy. There's something…show-offy about it."

Vanessa was surprised; she'd been thinking the same exact thing not long ago. "Kind of 'Look at me, look at how much money I have.'"

"Mama would sniff and call it 'puttin' on airs,' like a lady wearing her pocketbook on her back."

"Mama has opinions."

He chuckled. "Lots of them. Here we are."

He indicated a small, well-traveled Subaru SUV and opened the passenger door for her. It had been a long time since a man had opened a door for her, and the feeling was strange…and kind of nice, she admitted. As she got in, she said, "Thank you."

"Most welcome."

"I live in Venice, by the way, a little east of Abbot Kinney Boulevard."

He nodded. "Not too far from my place. When we get close, point me in the right direction."

Vanessa wasn't always a great passenger, most of the

time not trusting others to get her to her destination safely, but as they drove along, she realized she could trust Jackson's driving. He maneuvered the car with ease, in control, relaxed but alert. He would get them there just fine.

Which freed her mind to go over the meeting with Ray. She was so pleased with Shannon, who had taken on Constantine with aplomb. But far from pleased with the outcome and the way Ray had left it. What would he do next? she couldn't help wondering. And would she be ready when he did?

"Mind if I put on some music?"

Jackson's question startled her. "Oh. No, of course not."

She was surprised to hear something classical fill the car. A full orchestra with a soaring string line that was both exciting and soothing too. She had no idea who the composer was; she fully intended to take a music-appreciation class one day, so she wouldn't feel so completely ignorant. She found her shoulders loosening up, realizing she didn't need to think about Ray anymore, not tonight at least. She let the music wash over her, and she took in and expelled a deep breath.

Then she turned to the man next to her. "Thank you, by the way."

"For what?"

"Being there tonight. That was very generous of you."

When he gave a no-big-deal shrug, she added, "And for the flowers. They're lovely."

Now he glanced her way with a quick, almost shy, smile. "You liked them?"

"Very much."

She went back to staring out the window, noting cars going by, people hurrying on their way. After a while she broke the silence again. "I don't date."

"Okay."

"Like I said, I don't have time."

"Okay."

"But the flowers were beautiful."

"So you said."

Jackson just plum couldn't figure the woman out, and that was the truth.

During their one previous phone conversation, she'd been on the chilly side. When she'd first seen him tonight, she'd been surprised and again not pleased...at first, anyway. He hadn't known whether it was personal or because of the stress of meeting with Ray again. As Shannon had filled him on the details of the Garner-Ortiz connection, she'd remained silent and watchful.

Now as she sat next to him in the car, he sensed some inner tightness slowly uncoiling. If she wasn't being exactly warm to him, she was, at least, treating him like a human being.

A human being who didn't date, he reminded himself. Mental note: believe what she's saying, not what you wish she was saying.

But, dammit, he was still taken with her. He wanted her, and that was at the most primitive level, man to woman. Even in her no-nonsense navy-blue skirt and pale-green blouse, little gold hoops in her pretty ears, she radiated enough sensuality to heat a small room. Whenever she turned to face him, he got lost in those wide Mediterranean-colored eyes of hers, wanted to capture those full lips with his, wanted to stroke his hands all over her slim but curvy body.

Yet he kept it to himself. He was way past the age of panting and drooling. Besides, he'd decided to let the Fates fall where they decided to fall. He'd done all he could, he'd called, sent flowers, made his desire to see more of her known. The next move, if there was one— and he sincerely hoped there would be, even if he doubted his hope would be answered—was up to her.

She lived on a long block of older, bordering-on-shabby apartment buildings. Pointing to one in the middle of the block, she said, "That's me. You can drop me off."

Drop me off.

Okay, Jackson thought. There would be no next move. The End.

But he never "dropped off" a woman; not in his nature. "I see a parking space. I'll walk you to the door."

"That's not necessary."

"Humor me," he said firmly.

At least, he noted as they approached her building, the front door required a key, so there was some security. Although not enough to keep out anyone who really wanted in. And it looked as though that alleyway right next to the building led to the rear. Was there a secure back door? In this neighborhood, he somehow doubted it.

He watched as she inserted her key in the lock, then turned to face him. This was it, he was sure. The kiss-off. He braced himself.

Instead, she surprised him. "Would you like to come in? The kids should have supper ready. You're welcome to join us. It's the least I can do to thank you properly for tonight."

"You don't owe me anything."

"I would feel better."

"If you don't owe someone?"

"Yes."

He studied her for a moment, even as a voice inside his head was screaming, *Say yes, idiot.* Then he smiled. "What I ought to do is leave, so you'll still owe me," he said, but added quickly, "However, I'll accept your kind offer. I'd enjoy eating supper with you and your family."

As they entered the apartment, which opened onto a small foyer and right into the kitchen, the first thing he saw were his flowers, sitting on a round table. It pleased him no end, but he kept his face from breaking out into a huge grin. *Thank you, Mac,* he said silently.

The kitchen was small but welcoming, one whole side opening up to a living room with a hallway leading off to what he supposed were the bedrooms and bath.

Vanessa shouted, "Kids? I'm home. And I don't smell anything. Thomas? It was your turn."

"I put it in the oven," came from somewhere in the rear of the apartment.

"But you have to turn the oven on," she said, doing so.

Running feet preceded the entrance of the two boys he'd seen the day of the award presentation. The younger and shorter of the two made a face. "Oh, Mom. I'm sorry."

She rubbed the hair on the top of his head. "It's okay, honey. We'll just have to eat a little later."

Before she completed her sentence, both boys had

shifted their attention to Jackson. The expression in their eyes said they weren't sure what to make of this newcomer.

Vanessa said, "We're having a guest for dinner this evening. This is Detective Sergeant Jackson Rutherford." She turned to him with a small smile. "Have I got that right?"

The side of his mouth quirked up. "Yes, ma'am."

"You might remember him from when I got that award a couple of weeks ago. He was sitting on the stage with me? This is my oldest, Shane, then there's Thomas."

He offered his hand and one by one the boys shook it, still looking at him with suspicion.

The older of the two, Shane, who had earphones dangling around his long neck, was pretty skinny but must have had a recent growth spurt because his jeans were a little too short for his long legs. He had light tan skin, medium-brown hair, worn longish and shaggy, and a broad nose. Like his mother's his eyes, pale hazel in his case, had a very slight Asian cast to them. The other one, Thomas, was still in the baby-fat stage and more cheerful than his brother. He was light-skinned, his thick, curly hair and eyes very dark.

"Mommy!"

A little girl came running into the kitchen. "Mommy, you're home!" she said, hugging Vanessa around the legs. Then she gazed up at Jackson, her dark eyes wide with wonder. "You're big. Are you a giant?"

"No, I'm not, young lady. Just big for my age."

"This is Katy," Vanessa said, her hand on her daughter's head.

The child looked the most Hispanic of all the

children, with Ray's nearly black eyes and thick, straight, dark hair. You could see the stamp of the mother on all their faces. There was no doubt, Jackson thought, that Vanessa's brood was the original rainbow coalition.

"I'm six," Katy told him. "Will you lift me up? Please?"

"Katy," Vanessa admonished her.

"It's okay," Jackson said easily. He swooped down and lifted her into his arms. She was powder-puff light.

"See how tall I am, Shane?" Katy boasted. "I'm taller than you now."

The older boy shot his sister a bored look, gave a surly shrug, then adjusted his earphones and walked off.

"Did you get your homework done?" Vanessa asked his retreating back. When he didn't respond, she marched up to him and plucked the phones off his head.

Shane whirled around. "What?"

"I asked if you got your homework done."

"Yes. Okay? It's all done. Now may I have them back?" He held out his hand.

She looked, Jackson figured, as though she might like to have a little discussion about manners, but with company in the room, she kept her mouth shut. She handed him the phones, then turned with an apologetic smile to Jackson.

"I'm sorry. It will be an hour before dinner is ready. If you'd like to come back another time, I'd understand."

"No problem. Can I help?"

"No, thanks. Can I offer you anything to drink?"

"Got a beer?"

"No alcohol in the house, sorry."

"A soft drink'll do."

She went to the refrigerator, took out a can of soda and handed it to him. "Sit down, make yourself comfortable. Katy, you come help me with dinner."

As Jackson made his way toward the small living room, Thomas called out, "Hey, Shane. Come on. Let's throw the ball."

He might have had trouble hearing his mother, but Shane obviously had no such problem with his brother because he ambled from the rear of the apartment shortly afterward, a football tucked under his arm. The boys headed for the kitchen, and seconds later Jackson heard the sound of the back door slamming.

Sipping his soda, he walked around the small living room, checked out family pictures and shelves of used-looking books. After a while the smell from the kitchen had his mouth watering, and he headed in that direction, noting how Vanessa maneuvered around her little girl with enormous patience. "Sure I can't help?" he offered again.

"Positive."

He made his way to the back door, saying, "In that case, I'm gonna get me some night air."

He opened the door and stepped out. It was dark, but a series of lights illuminated a long alleyway that stretched from one block to the next, lined with open carports on one side and apartment house rear doors on the other. The two boys were tossing a football ball back and forth. He stood there, watching them for a few minutes before saying, "How 'bout I throw the ball to both of you?"

"No, thanks," Shane said.

"Cool," Thomas said.

Jackson waited. Then Shane shrugged. "Okay, whatever."

That young man was not happy with his appearance on the scene. As the oldest, he probably felt the most protective of his mother. Couldn't blame him. Shane just needed a little time to get used to him, was all.

He was tossed the ball, which felt good in his hands. It had been a while. College, when he'd been a tight end. "Okay," he said, waving them farther and farther back. "Here we go." He let loose with a long, high, lazy spiral.

The small window next to the back door was open and, in the kitchen, Vanessa could hear hoots and laughter from the alleyway as Jackson played with her sons. From what she could tell, all of them were having a great time.

Who was this man? And what in the world had she done? Why had she invited Jackson to dinner? It had just tumbled out of her mouth before she'd stopped to think. Now, remembering the look on Shane's face, she reminded herself that she had a rule about inviting new men home, which was that she didn't. Not ever.

So how had she allowed this hulking, Southern-accented, scary-looking cop to get his foot in the door? One moment she was adamantly turning him down for coffee, the next, she was impulsively inviting him for dinner. Now her boys were acting like a long-lost daddy had been sent from heaven.

The truth was, she didn't really get Jackson Rutherford. Or she couldn't really pigeonhole him, anyway. He seemed easygoing but she'd seen the capacity for violence when he'd dealt with Ray. He had this Southern accent and was built like a Mac truck, but he listened to classical music and he had beautiful eyes.

What did he want from her?

Sex, for sure. What a surprise, she thought wryly. She'd seen his glances of appreciation when he thought she wasn't looking. With her background, she had built-in radar when it came to men and their interest in her. If he wanted in her pants, though, the poor man was out of luck. No man had been there since she got off drugs, and she wasn't looking to change that. Men—all of them— had that single track their brains ran on, the one located beneath their belts, and Jackson was no different.

As soon as he found out that as far as she was concerned this particular track led to a dead end, he would take off like a bat out of hell.

Which was fine with her.

Really, just fine.

Chapter 4

*S*imilar. *Empathy. Youth. Help.*

Jackson put the tiles in place right under the *p* from *help*, to spell *psyche.*

Vanessa glanced up at him. "You're really good at this."

"Back atcha."

"You're both way too good for me," Thomas griped. It was his turn next and he stared at his tiles with displeasure.

Katy was in bed. Vanessa, Jackson, Shane and Thomas were gathered around the Scrabble set, which was laid out on the clean kitchen table. Thomas had been the one to invite Jackson to join them in their weekly game, a tradition Vanessa had begun after reading an article about getting kids to enjoy "the romance of words," through Scrabble.

While Shane and Thomas studied their letters, Vanessa said to Jackson, "No, I mean it. Your vocabulary is amazing."

One side of his mouth quirked up. "You surprised at that?"

"Not really. I mean…"

"You didn't expect a large vocabulary from, what? A good ol' Southern boy? A hard-ass cop? Pardon my language, boys."

Thomas snickered while Shane rolled his eyes upward.

Now she felt embarrassed, even though Jackson's teasing seemed good-natured. "I actually don't know what I meant. I think it has something to do with…the brains versus brawn thing. I mean, look at you. Someone who obviously spends so much time working out…"

Oh, God, now she'd gone from insulting him to letting him know she was aware of his body.

"…doesn't have the time or inclination to develop his mind?" he said, finishing her sentence for her with a chuckle.

She winced. "I guess I'm guilty of stereotyping. Sorry."

"It's one of the classic ones," he said easily. "And I don't spend all that much time working out. I go to the gym a couple of times a week, run on the beach some mornings. The men in my family are all pretty big. And my vocabulary is thanks to my mama. I was raised by a woman who does at least one crossword puzzle every day of her life."

"Got it. And I'm still impressed. Using the *h* in *handle* to form *plethora*. Wow."

"How about your making *term* into *termagant*," he countered. "Talk about impressive."

She'd been pretty proud of that one herself. "I've always been fascinated by new words. I love to read."

"Mom always has a book with her in her purse," Thomas offered. "She says you have to wait a lot in life, so reading makes the time go faster. There," he added, laying out his letters to spell *endure*.

"Good one, Thomas," Vanessa said. "How are you doing, Shane?"

"He took my *e*," her oldest said with a scowl.

"Guess you'll have to find another word."

"Yeah. Easy for you to say." He glanced up at Jackson, whom he had treated with a watchful distance most of the evening. "Mom keeps a dictionary next to her bed."

"Can you believe that?" Thomas piped in. "She reads the dictionary for *fun*."

Jackson nodded. "Hey, we all need our fun…however and wherever we can get it."

It was a perfectly innocent observation, Vanessa knew, but all evening, throughout dinner and during most of this game, he'd been coming up with little remarks that had definite double meanings. He always looked blandly innocent when he did, which was the giveaway. She shot him a look that let him know she was on to him.

Jackson, who dwarfed the normal-size chair, leaned back, looking perfectly at home. "I checked out your library earlier," he said. "What do you prefer to read… beside the dictionary?"

She shrugged. "Mysteries, romances, biographies. When I get the time away from schoolwork."

"What are you studying?"

"Just getting my college degree, slowly, at night. It's going to take forever."

"Mom's going to be a counselor one day," Thomas said. "She says she wouldn't be here today if others hadn't helped her, so she wants to give back."

"Thomas, hush. The detective doesn't need to know everything about me."

"Don't mind hearing it," Jackson said with a smile.

"Yes!" Shane set down an s after *play*, then spelled out *smelly*. He punched his fist in the air. "And that's a triple on the *y*."

Thomas, the tip of his tongue jutting out of the corner of his mouth, used a calculator to add up the new scores. "Okay, it's Detective Rutherford first, Mom second, Shane right behind her and me last," he said good-naturedly. "But that's only because I'm the youngest. I'll beat you all when I grow up."

"A fine goal." Jackson stood, stretched, reminding Vanessa once again of just how huge the man was. "I better get going. Got an early day tomorrow."

"What time do you start?" she asked.

"Six."

Shane made a face. "Man, that's way too early."

"I'm going to walk Jackson to the door," Vanessa said. "You put everything away, okay, boys?"

"Good night," Jackson said, offering his hand to Thomas.

The younger of the two boys shook it eagerly, Jackson noted. The kid's hormones, and the personality change usually associated with their onset, hadn't yet kicked in. He was still open and had a natural sweetness to his nature. Shane, on the other hand, still eyed him with suspicion as he grudgingly shook hands. He would take some winning over.

He'd had a similar thought earlier, Jackson realized. Which meant, he further realized, that he was planning on doing this a lot—being with Vanessa and her family, in her life. Now, just when had he come to that decision?

And was it even a wise one?

They left the apartment and she walked him to the building's front door, where they stopped. He smiled down at her; without her heels, she was a little thing. "Thanks for dinner. You are one fine cook."

She seemed pleased with the compliment. "Thank *you* for being there today. And again for the flowers."

"Way too many thanks. Consider yourself off the hook now. We're even."

"Oh, no," she said, her eyes widening. "I didn't mean—"

"Just funnin' with you. I know what you meant."

His hand had a mind of its own because, out of nowhere, it reached up and stroked her cheek, something he'd been wanting to do all evening. Her skin was, as he'd expected, soft. Warm to the touch, too.

She seemed startled by his action, and her mouth opened slightly in shock. But she didn't pull away. So, cupping her chin, he bent over and brushed his mouth over hers. Just once.

That one, brief connection to her sexy mouth was enough to light a small flame inside him; what he wanted to do now was to kiss her again, longer and deeper this time, do a little exploring.

Instead he held himself back, met her still-surprised gaze. "So now you know," he said softly. "I want to see more of you. Let me know if you feel the same. Good night, Vanessa."

With what he hoped was a jaunty smile, he walked out the door. Once outside, he sucked in a gutful of cool night air, which he sorely needed. Man, the woman turned him on something fierce! One moment of skin on skin and his hormones were jumping like fleas near a fire.

Pondering just what he'd set in motion, he made his way to his car. For sure the evening had turned out way differently than he'd expected. If he were totally honest with himself—which he always tried to be—he'd admit that the driving force behind his interest in Vanessa Garner had been, up until tonight, his physical attraction to her. That first time he'd seen her, the part of him that functioned as a primal animal looking to mate had responded eagerly.

Then he'd heard some of her story and a grudging respect had been added to the mix. Seeing her barreling out of the lawyer's office earlier this evening, all enraged and mama-bear protective, then sharing dinner with her family—each new event added to the layers of complexity in the woman. At some point she'd stopped being an object of raw desire—well, stopped being that primarily—and become a three-D, bona fide human being.

But that physical urge was still there; hell, he was human too, wasn't he? That little kiss at the door had reminded him of that very fact in no uncertain terms. And so he'd let her know there could be more of that kind of thing and left it up to her.

And he had no idea what she'd do, none at all. Did she want him nearly as much as he wanted her? Man, he sure hoped so.

Or did he?

Jackson scratched his head. This was a potential mine field. He couldn't just get the woman into bed and let an affair run its course. She wasn't the short-term affair type. She had kids. Hell, she also had a lot of other baggage. Not for the first time, he told himself to look at this with wide-open eyes. No matter how much progress Vanessa Garner had made, she was the mother of three kids from three different daddies, a reformed drug addict and, in the past, an occasional hooker. How did he feel about that?

Not to mention that she and her offspring had enough ethnicity in their bloodstreams to pose for a chart representing the entire world and all its peoples—another element to ponder. Sure, he was a product of his background who had tried to stretch and grow enough to get past the color of a person's skin before making his mind up about them. But the truth was he never *had* lived in a lily-white world, so, unless he was kidding himself, it wasn't Vanessa's racial makeup that was in the way.

No, it was the fact of her. He was a practical man. He had a life plan, goals he was working toward. Vanessa Garner came with way too many responsibilities, not to mention ghosts. If he wasn't ready or willing to take that on, all of it, well then why start something that had nowhere to go? And, yeah, she had the sexiest voice and the softest mouth in the history of the universe. So what? There were lots of soft mouths out there, and they didn't come with a ready-made family and enough tawdry history to fill a shrink's entire practice.

He'd done the right thing by leaving it up to her. Most likely she wouldn't contact him, which would make his life a hell of a lot easier. If just a little bit less interesting.

Vanessa finished chopping the garlic and added it to the pan, appreciating the smells surrounding her small kitchen. Cooking for her family was always one of the best times of the week. Not only did she have a dictionary next to her bed, but she usually had a cookbook or two that she'd picked up at her favorite used bookstore. When she found a recipe that intrigued her, she often tried it out on the kids, with modifications, of course, having to do with the taste buds of three children of varying ages and her own budget. Tonight was something with bulgur and chicken legs.

Jackson had praised her cooking, which had warmed her at the time. That had been nearly a week ago, and there'd been no word from him since. Not that she'd expected one—she was, apparently, to call him. Right.

The same amount of time had passed since the meeting at the lawyer's office. Ray wasn't done with her, that she knew, but he was usually so impatient when he wanted something, this was unusual. Shannon had reported no communication from Constantine, either. Had Ray actually seen that there was no possibility he'd get his way this time?

Either way, the not knowing had her on edge. That first shoe had dropped; all week she'd been poised waiting for the thud of the other one.

The ringing of the doorbell interrupted her musings.

After turning down the heat under the pan, she wiped her hands on a dish towel as she walked over to the front door. She punched in the old-fashioned speaker. "Yes? Who is it?"

"UPS. I have packages for Katy, Shane and Thomas Garner."

Frowning, she pushed the buzzer to allow him in, then waited to look through the eyehole to make sure the man at the door really was who he said he was. Sure enough, brown uniform, three packages of varying sizes. Who could have sent them? she wondered. Aunt Lupe? Maybe the women from A Single Voice? A fleeting thought that it might be Jackson came to her mind, but she immediately dismissed that one. Flowers were nice, gifts for the children would be excessive. Especially as he hadn't even called.

She opened the door and signed for the packages, after which she called out, "Kids? It looks like you have some presents here."

From all over the apartment they came running. The boxes were taken into the living room where each one ripped open their presents with excitement.

Shane found his treasure first, pulling out an Xbox with all the accessories. "Wow," he said softly, wide-eyed wonder on his face, an expression she hadn't seen in a couple of years.

Next was a sleek silver Game Boy for Thomas, who grinned from ear to ear. "Mom! This is so cool!" he said.

There were three Barbie dolls and lots of dresses for Katy.

All of them ignored the small gift card that came with

their presents, and as she picked up one of them, Vanessa had a sudden sick feeling in the pit of her stomach. Her intuition had been right; sure enough, all the gifts were from Ray, and the knowledge chilled her to the bone. The other shoe had dropped. He wasn't done with her yet. Not by a long shot.

Katy, her dark eyes bright with happiness, looked up from her brand-new Elina Barbie. "It's not my birthday, Mommy. Who gave us this stuff?"

"Ray," Vanessa said dully.

"Who's Ray?" she said, happily tearing at box after box of Barbie goodies.

"Yeah," Thomas chimed in, running his hand lovingly over the top of the Game Boy before opening it up. "Who is Ray?"

Only Shane's expression changed to a frown. "Ray?" he said.

She met his gaze. "Yes. And I'm sorry, but we can't accept these."

"Huh?" Thomas said.

She had to swallow down a lump in her throat before going on. "I said we can't accept these gifts. Put them back in their boxes. Now." It came out more sharply than she had intended.

Katy instantly burst into tears. "But…but, my Barbies!" she wailed.

Vanessa could see the anger on Shane's face. Even Thomas, her good-natured mamma's boy, turned mutinous. "But, Mom…"

"I'm sorry. I really am. I wish I could afford to buy these for you, I really do."

"Why are you crying, Mommy?" Katy asked.

She swiped a finger across her lower lid. "It's okay. Just, please. We can't take these."

"But why?" Thomas asked.

"Because they're from Ray, doofus." It was Shane who spoke this, his eyes hard.

Her oldest child knew about Ray because he'd been nearly eight when Vanessa had been pregnant with Katy, and even though both boys had been living with Lupe at that time, Vanessa visited with them as often as she could. Shane had observed her bruises every time Ray beat her, he'd heard her crying to Aunt Lupe the times she'd tried to leave him. Thomas, who had been five and half at the time, seemed to have very little memory of those days. He'd either been too young or had blocked it all out.

But not Shane. Shane got it right away.

Even so, he gazed at the Xbox with naked yearning in his eyes. "Why did he send them?" he asked.

"To win you over," she said softly. "To make you not listen to me. He figured he could bribe you."

"What does bribe mean?" Katy asked, her cheeks wet with disappointed tears.

"It's when you really, really don't want to do something and someone else offers you money or a present to get you to change your mind."

She sniffed. "Like when I get my allowance for making my bed?"

"Like that, but more serious. Please. Put them back, all of you. Ray is trouble, big-time trouble. He knows I don't want him anywhere near you, any of you. If you really want these things, let's try to come up with a plan on how to get them. Maybe we can start a savings account. Okay?"

One by one, she met the eyes of each of her children. They were deeply disappointed, not at all pleased with her or the situation, but they did as she requested. Sullenly they put their presents back their containers. Tomorrow she would drop them off on the way to work.

Ray, she thought, hating him all over again. That miserable excuse for a human being. Fear and intimidation, lawyers and bribes. And now gifts for her kids. Showing what a good guy he was, how he could give Katy a much better life than her mother could afford. He really didn't get it and he never would. But he also wouldn't give up.

A shiver of fear melted the hate. How far would Ray go to get what he wanted? God! She felt so alone, having to be the bad guy, having to disappoint her kids, who really didn't have a lot and really never asked for much. Sometimes she wondered if she was being fair to them, trying to do it all, to keep them all together, struggling with every penny she earned. Again that sense of desolation, of sheer loneliness, hit her like a wave.

Jackson. Out of nowhere, he was there in her head.

Which wasn't hard to figure out why. Raising these kids by herself sometimes led to thoughts that it would be nice to have a man to lean on, to depend on, to back her up when she had to be stern, to set boundaries. And Jackson was the most recent man to have entered her life.

And exited it pretty quickly. She felt a spurt of annoyance with him. After that nice dinner, why hadn't he at least called to say thank you?

Maybe he simply wasn't interested.

No, she'd seen the interest. Well, sexual interest for sure. And if anyone knew the signs, she did. Since age eleven and her early development, men had been sniffing around her. She had the "musk," Aunt Lupe used to say with a mixture of humor and sadness.

Lupe wasn't really her aunt, but the sister of one of her mother's boyfriends. Vanessa and she had formed a bond early on, and after the boyfriend was history, Lupe made an effort to stay in Vanessa's life. Over the years, she'd become an integral part of it. A surrogate mother, actually, considering the fact that Vanessa had received very little mothering of her own. A much-loved surrogate mother, to her kids as well as to her.

The "musk," Aunt Lupe had told her, meant that she would never lack for attention from men, and that was, depending on circumstances, either the good news or the bad.

Vanessa had had plenty of bad from it, thank you, beginning with the rape at age fourteen and ending with Ray six years ago. Since then she'd firmly cut off any and all overtures from any interested men.

And she would continue to do so, including Jackson. If he ever called. Which he probably would not. One thing she knew for sure was she was not about to call him.

Jackson clicked through the TV channels, restless for something to distract him. He'd been pretty busy the past few days. They were on the verge of getting a major dealer off the streets before he could get any more ten-year-olds hooked and peddling for him. The last of the paperwork was on his desk, awaiting him in the morning; so were calls to the witnesses he and Sal had lined up.

But it wasn't the case he needed distracting from. It was Vanessa. She was in his head. Twenty-four/seven, as a matter of fact, for days now. He wanted to see her; hell, he just plain *wanted* her. Bad. And no amount of talking to himself about all the drawbacks of being with her were working. Her presence in his head just kept getting stronger and stronger.

The phone rang. He glanced at his watch. Nearly ten. He picked up the cordless phone next to the couch. "Yes?"

"Hello."

His heart stopped. Literally stopped. The woman had called!

"Hey, Vanessa." He turned the TV to mute. "How's it going?"

There was a slight hesitation on the other end of the line before she said, "All right, I guess."

Something in her voice was off. He sat up straighter. "Tell me. What's going on? You heard from Ray?"

"Indirectly. He sent presents for the kids, and I'm not going to let them keep them, so I'm not real popular around here."

"Damn. That must be tough."

She sighed. "Yes. It…gets kind of lonely sometimes. I'm sorry, I didn't mean to sound so self-pitying."

"Not at all," he reassured her. "Hey, we all get lonely sometimes. If that's why you called, I'm fine with it."

"Well, yes, that's one of the reasons I called. But the other was to tell you why I *haven't* called."

"Okay," he said slowly, not sure he was going to like what came next.

"The thing is, Jackson," she began, still sounding a little shaky, "we, the kids and I, have this safe little world. It stays that way because I don't bring any men into it. It can get, well, complicated. How long will they be around? Should the kids get attached or shouldn't they? We've had such a rocky time of it—you have no idea, really, none."

"No, I don't."

"It's taken me so long and so much hard work to get to this place," she went on, all traces of hesitation gone now, "but we're good, the kids and I. Well, except for the usual stuff, but you know what I mean. I'm afraid to introduce a new element into it. It all seems so...fragile." She let out another long sigh. "And I've just told you a lot more about myself and my life than I ever planned on doing."

He allowed himself a small smile. "I'm honored you did. So that's why you called? To tell me you don't want to see me?"

"Yes."

"Hey, darlin', all you had to do was *not* call. I would have gotten the message."

She didn't answer.

He let a beat go by before saying, "Let's cut to the chase, okay? Is it me?"

"Is what you?"

"Is it me you don't want to see? Me, specifically?"

She took way too long to answer. "Maybe. In a way."

Hoo, boy. He hadn't seen that one coming. Right to the solar plexus. But he'd asked. "Okay. I get it."

"No, wait. I don't mean that I don't…like you. I mean, I find you…interesting. If I did want to date I would want to date you…I think."

His laugh was rueful. "What's the expression? 'Damned with faint praise'?"

"Well, look. We're so different. From such different backgrounds."

"You mean racially?"

"That, yes. And economically. And regionally. Your mother did crossword puzzles, mine drank a fifth of scotch a day. I have no idea who my father was. Not to mention the fact that you're a cop and I don't have a very good history with the police—they've never been in my corner."

That one made him bristle. "I'm not *the* police."

"Okay, fine," she said, sounding a little irritated with him, too. "I'm guilty of stereotyping again, got it."

"And not just about cops. And sorry, but I don't buy the 'We're too different' excuse. You want a clone of yourself? Because I surely don't want one of myself. I'd bore me to tears in a week."

He took a moment to put it on simmer, to stop feeling defensive, before going on. "Come on, Vanessa. Take a chance. Come out to dinner with me."

Another pause. Then, "I honestly don't know when."

At this sign that her attitude was softening, his heart took a little leap. "Nothin' fancy. An hour, hour and a half. Just us. No kids. Although," he added quickly, "I like your kids."

Her quiet chuckle warmed him some more, as did her throaty voice when she said, "You are persistent, aren't you?"

"When I want something, yes, ma'am."

A long sigh let him know he'd won. Yes! "Okay. Tonight's what? Wednesday? Lupe has the kids over to dinner on Thursday nights. I get off work at six tomorrow and my class starts at eight. That's the window."

"Where's your job?"

"Culver City."

"And your school?"

"In Santa Monica."

"You like Japanese noodles? Ramen?"

"Love it."

"Good. Meet me tomorrow night at Yokohama Ramen, corner Barrington and Gateway. As close to six as you can make it."

She was running late; she'd had to do a couple of interviews for a new receptionist, as Renee had taken off with a man she'd met at a rave and had neglected to formally quit. Vanessa was exhausted from trying to find someone who could actually speak whole sentences and get messages straight.

It was a modest restaurant located in a modest corner mall, and Jackson was already seated at a corner table when she arrived. When he stood and pulled her chair out for her, she sat, grateful for the gesture. Today he wore a white dress shirt open at the neck, its sleeves rolled up to the elbows, revealing tanned, muscular forearms. A brown jacket hung over the back of his chair. His hair was growing in, she observed. When they'd first met it had been very short. And he still had that very attractive stubble shadowing his jawline.

A Japanese brand beer bottle and chilled glass were in front of him. "Get you a drink?" he asked her.

"I don't drink. But I'd love some water."

As he signaled the waiter he asked, "Do you mind if I drink?"

"Not at all."

She waited a beat for the next question, then gave him points for not probing further. "Since I got off the drugs, I find it's better not to get into any substance that alters the mind. It could be dangerous."

He nodded, ordered her a bottle of designer water and indicated the menu on the table in front of her. "Let's get the food out of the way so we have time to visit."

"I want a big bowl of noodles, pork and vegetables. Would you mind ordering for me? I've made enough decisions today."

"Got it." When the waiter came back with her water, Jackson took care of ordering. Then he took a long draw of his beer, set it down and favored her with a small smile. His eyes were really very blue. "So."

"So."

"Here we are." His smiled broadened. "Should I say 'finally'?"

"You could." A fluttery sensation in the pit of her stomach took her by surprise. She'd found it pretty easy to talk to Jackson so far, but now they were actually sitting across the table from each other, no kids, no purpose other than to be together. And she was more drawn to him than she'd allowed herself to admit, up till now.

"Are you just a tad skittish?" he asked. "Because I am."

She laughed with relief at his welcome honesty. "Not

anymore." She raised her water glass. "To getting together. Finally, as you say."

He clinked. "Our first official date."

And last? she wondered. When he found out she really wasn't interested in sex, probably so.

They spent the time until the food came filling in some blanks. She learned that Jackson was enrolled for the fall in law school, planning to attend nights, with no clear goal in mind, just options for when he retired from the force in a few years. He'd gone to Birmingham Southern College for two years, then joined the Marines, finishing his degree while serving Uncle Sam. He'd seen action in the Middle East.

"Were you in actual battles?" she asked. "Were you hurt?"

"Yes and no. I was lucky. Others weren't." There was a small pause and she realized it was an area he didn't want to pursue. "When I came back, my tour of duty was over and I didn't re-up. Came out to the Golden State. Joined the police force."

"Why here? Why California?"

He shrugged. "Suits my personality." When she had to smile at that one, he shot her a mock-insulted glare. "What's so funny?"

"I have no idea what you mean by that."

"What, I don't have a personality?"

"On the contrary. You have a very strong personality. It just doesn't seem, well, particularly Californian."

"And what does a typically Californian personality look like?"

That made her pause and consider. "I'm thinking in

stereotypes again, aren't I? I meant laid-back, not overly ambitious, in the sun all day."

"Are you like that?"

"No."

"Do you know anyone like that?"

"Not really. I see them down at the beach. You know, the surfer dudes, the kids hanging out on the boardwalk with boom boxes and iPods."

"Well, sure, all the sunshine can do that to you, leech out the energy, if you have nothing better to do. Most of us do, though."

Out of nowhere, he picked up her hand and rubbed the skin of her knuckles with his thumb. "But no, what I mean about it suits my personality is the way no one forces you to conform to what they think you ought to be or do. There's a sense of personal freedom out here that I like."

Her skin felt warmed by his touch, which was gentle and firm at the same time. Her cheeks felt kind of warm, too.

"Who was trying to make you conform?" she asked.

He shrugged. "Pretty much my whole family. My daddy had a very successful insurance company and dabbled in local politics before he died. Mama wanted me to follow in his shoes, give luster to the 'glorious Rutherford name.'"

"You didn't agree."

Now he was rubbing each finger separately, a kind of gentle massage that felt delicious, soothing…and tingly at the same time.

"Mama and I don't agree on a lot of things. Don't get

me wrong, she's a great gal and I love her, but she's *very* traditional and set in her ways."

The sensations from her hand were beginning to spread to other parts of her body now; she felt her nipples growing hard, her breathing shallower. It was difficult to get her next words out. "So you came here to get away from your mother?" she managed.

"Not really. If you solve a problem by moving away from it, you just take it with you. No, I came here because of what I said about it suiting me, and because when I was eight we traveled from San Francisco to San Diego by car, one summer vacation, and I always knew I'd come back. And my mouth's flapping enough to catch flies. I'm not usually this talkative."

"The strong, silent type?"

"Well, more silent than I am with you, for sure. Your turn."

The food came then and she retrieved her hand from his, grateful that something external had given her the excuse, because on her own she didn't know if she had the strength. The sensations his touch had set off had shocked her. It had been seven years since she'd been with a man.

And a lot longer since she'd enjoyed it.

She glanced at her watch. "I have to eat fast and get out of here."

His smile was understanding, and just a little knowing. The man was a master at reading women, she figured. But it didn't matter, she told herself. When he found out, he would go on his merry way.

Jackson picked up on Vanessa's uneasiness as he

walked her to her car after dinner. He knew his little hand and finger massage had gotten to her—was she not real happy it had? When they got to her car, she played nervously with her keys, then looked up at him.

"Thanks for the dinner, Jackson. It was delicious."

He patted his stomach. "I'm full as a tick on a hound dog myself." When she smiled before inserting her key in the lock, he added, "And I want us to do this some more."

She didn't reply, didn't open her door. It was like she was thinking, considering, waiting.

So he put a hand on her shoulder, turned her around and cupped her face in his hands. Good Lord, her eyes were something else, the color of a deep-turquoise stone shot through with light; a man could drown in them. He leaned over and kissed her, this time thrusting his tongue through her generous lips right away, so the message was clear. And after a couple of moments, she opened wider and thrust her tongue back.

He got lost then, in the taste of her, the juice of her, the smell of her. Lemons from her hair, sweet, spicy sauce from the dinner. And something more, something that reminded him of a hot, tropical evening. Moving his hand to the back of her head, he angled it so he could go deeper. At the sound of her soft groan of response, he felt his organ coming to attention. Like that. Instant turn-on.

She broke away from the kiss, averting her head. "No. Please don't."

He released her. "All right," he managed to say. The kiss, the very textures of her, had robbed him of his breath.

Chest heaving, Vanessa gazed at him out of uncertain eyes, licked her lips. "Jackson, it's not going to happen."

"What isn't?"

"Us, sleeping together."

He nodded. "Fine."

"Fine?"

"Yes."

She darted a quick glance down to the prominent bulge behind his jeans zipper, then quickly looked away. "Um, I may be stating the obvious," she said with a nervous little laugh, "but, well, you're a man."

"Glad you noticed," he said wryly.

"And it's hard—" She put a hand over her face. "Oh, God." She lowered her hand. "I mean *difficult* to miss the signs that, well, it's not so fine that we stopped."

"Hey, I'm a grown-up. I can wait."

"I said it's not going to happen."

"Tonight?"

"Ever."

"Really? You got some kind of crystal ball?"

She shook her head, as though she had no idea what to do with the way he was reacting. "I mean it. I'm done with all that."

"'All that.'" he quoted her musingly, then leaned against her car door, crossed his arms and nodded. "Hey, with what I know about your past, Vanessa, I get it. But, see, I got me a theory. And that theory is that we get to reinvent ourselves every seven years. So your past? That life? It's gone. Vaporized. You are a whole other person now." He smiled at her, pleased to see that she was listening to him with wonder on her face. "A young, beautiful woman, at the beginning of your young, beautiful life."

Her eyes filled, and he could tell she wasn't happy about it. "Damn you, Jackson. Why do you get to me this way?"

"I'd be willing to venture a guess."

"I don't want to hear it."

With an index finger, he wiped away a tear. "Some other time, then."

She punched him lightly in the chest. "And stop being so agreeable."

"Just can't win, now, can I?"

She laughed again, knuckled away the moisture on her cheek. "I don't know what I want."

"Well, I know what I want." He stroked her face, her soft, sweet cheek. "Haven't a doubt about it."

She sighed. "Message received," she said ruefully. "Loud and clear."

He pushed himself away from the car and planted a light kiss on her nose. Then he opened her car door, helped her into the driver's seat and handed her the keys. With one hand on the top of the door frame, he leaned in. "Go to school. And don't worry. I'm not going to rush things. Like I said, I'm a grown-up."

She glanced up at him. "This is your way of saying you're not going to take no for an answer, isn't it?"

"Yes, ma'am. It's my way of saying just that."

Chapter 5

"Shane! Are you going to keep that phone tied up all night?"

"All right, I heard you the first time," he called from the kitchen, clearly annoyed with his mother.

Well, she wasn't real thrilled with him, either. It was eight o'clock on a Friday evening, and Vanessa was in her bedroom, trying to study. *Trying* being the operative word, because all evening she'd had her ear on alert for the sound of a phone ringing. For her. From Jackson.

Except she wanted to ask him something, so why was she waiting for him to call her? Because, to be honest, she would feel better, more valued somehow, if he called her. Which was nonsense.

She picked up the receiver. Shane was still talking to this new girl—what was her name? Thomas had been teasing his older brother at the dinner table. Apparently Lanetta was history and now it was—? Calista? Kaneesha? Karista, that was it. With a *K*.

"I mean it, Shane," she said.

"Two minutes!"

"I'm sorry, but I've been waiting awhile already. Please tell your friend you need to say good-night. I'll give you *one* more minute."

As she set the receiver down she thought she'd probably broken some kind of sacred teenager privacy rule, but she was past caring. She had needs too. She glanced at her watch. Two minutes, no more.

Not half a minute later the phone rang and she picked it up. "Hello?"

"Hey, there."

Her heart gave a little surge. "Jackson?"

"None other. Your line's been busy."

"Three kids. One of these days I'll have to find the money to get a second line. Or maybe a cell phone."

"Good idea. Well, I just wanted to let you know I enjoyed being with you last night."

"Me, too. That was a great restaurant."

"Yeah. I'm really into Asian food—didn't get much of the real stuff back in Alabama. At least in my neck of the woods."

"Jackson, listen, it's good that you called because I wanted to invite you to a party."

"Really?" He sounded pleased.

"Yes. You remember my lawyer, Shannon? Well, she has this storefront place where they give free legal advice and advocacy—"

"The Last House on the Block," he cut in. "I've been there. Mac Marshall used to be my partner."

"Of course. I forgot."

"And your aunt Lupe is the receptionist. I met her a couple weeks back while I was visiting Mac. We got all kinds of connections, you and I."

"I guess we do. Anyway, they're having an anniversary party on Sunday afternoon, a kind of open house. Want to go with me and the kids?"

She'd gone over this in her mind. Part of her wanted to keep Jackson and whatever it was they had together separate and apart from the children. If they got too attached to him, when he left, well, it just wouldn't be fair. But part of her also needed him to understand that they were not only included in the package but that they came first. Most men would run screaming from her family situation. It would most likely send Jackson running into the night, too, and if it did, better to get rid of him now rather than later.

"I'm looking through my mail," he said, "which I haven't touched in a few days. And I see here an invite from Mac for the same affair. So, yes, of course. How's two on Sunday? We can all go in my car."

"I look forward to it." She hung up the phone, a pleased smile on her face, a small hum of pleasure in her heart.

The storefront had been spiffed up since he'd last seen it, Jackson noticed. The lettering across the now shiny-clean window had been done in gold, the door painted a bright, welcoming blue. The interior walls were a warm yellow and there were plants all around on every available space. Lupe's desk was spread with platters of cookies, crackers and cheese, and bowls of nuts. On another table there were champagne and sodas.

It was a crush, with people in the main room, people in Shannon's rear office, people spilling out onto the street. It was loud too, lots of conversation and laughter, some salsa music leaking through the noise.

When Lupe saw Jackson walking in with Vanessa and her kids, her face lit up and she threw open her arms. Each of the children and Vanessa got huge hugs. Then the older woman squinted up at him, head cocked to one side as though deciding. He leaned over and bussed her cheek. That had her opening her arms and giving him a hug, too.

Okay, he thought, *passed some kind of test.*

The minute the kids saw the food, they began to dig in. "Not too much," Vanessa cautioned. "Leave some for the other guests."

Lupe waved her hand. "We got plenty more. It's okay."

"You spoil them."

"It's my job."

He was introduced to all kinds of folks including Shannon's sister Carmen and her husband, J.R., Carmen and Shannon's mom, Grace. He met a homeless lady named Gidget, who remained outside but near, holding onto her shopping cart and a dog named Bonzo. He actually knew a couple of people there himself, like Mac's wife Wanda, who embraced him warmly, then darted her gaze from him to Vanessa, one eyebrow arched.

A smile creased her mahogany-colored face. "So? You two a couple or something?"

He slanted Vanessa a look. Instead of returning it, she said pointedly, "Let's go with 'or something.' We just came here together, that's all."

Mac, his arm around his wife, gave Jackson a thumbs-up gesture with his free hand. He smiled back, but inside he was wondering what was up. Vanessa was downplaying their being together, didn't want to be seen as a couple. Which, he supposed, was good, as he too didn't quite know what was up with them.

He remembered, back in the beginning, that there were a bunch of reasons on his part not to get serious—hell, not to even *start* with this woman—but lately he seemed to be barreling down a road with no inclination to turn around, and those really good, important reasons not to get serious about Vanessa were getting lost somewhere behind him.

Mental note: do some thinking about what you're starting here, Jackson. *Serious* thinking.

The noise was nearly overwhelming, but after a while the sound of a gavel being pounded on a desk made conversation cease. Shannon, being a pretty small person, was standing on the desk. When the room was quiet, she beamed at all of them.

"Thanks so much for coming today. It means a lot. Now, some of you know our story, how I had a dream from early on to start a place like this, how we opened two years ago, part-time, just me and Lupe—" clapping and cheers for her and Lupe, who waved "—and a couple of my lawyer friends whose arms I twisted to donate a few hours a week. J.R.—" who bowed in a mocking fashion "—and Revetta Johnson." A wave from a pretty African-American woman. "And how, through the gift of an anonymous benefactor we were able to open full-time a year ago."

Huge cheers made Shannon grin, but she signaled for silence before going on. "Many of you don't know how we got our name. Macklin Thurgood Marshall, Jr., our resident investigator—" cheers for Mac "—who came onboard full-time fourteen months ago, came up with it and he's going to tell you the story right now. Mac?"

"Do I have to get up on that desk?"

Chuckles. "Nope. You're over five feet, so wail away from down there."

Smiling, Mac gazed around the crowd, caught Jackson's eye, winked. In his deep bass voice, he began. "It's no secret to most of you that I am clean and sober in Alcoholics Anonymous for eight years. In AA, we got a lot of desperate people of all kinds. Poor people, middle-class people, rich people. Secret drinkers, public drinkers. Homeless old guys and pretty young teenage girls. When they come in the doors, like I say, they're desperate. They've been every place else. They've tried to stop by themselves, tried rehabs and shots and pills and therapists. Nothing has done the job. So when they walk in the door, they know there are no more places to go, no more chances. They've come to the last house on the block; in other words, this is it—get it here or die.

"A lot of our clients feel the same way when they come through our doors. They need some justice and they haven't been able to get it. They've spent their last dime on lawyers who failed them. The entire legal system has failed them. So have the cops, the government, social workers, shrinks, you name it. So we're here. The last best hope between our clients and despair." He raised his glass of club soda. "To Shannon and her dream. To all of you who work here and volunteer here. To the Last House on the Block. Long may she thrive."

Jackson joined in the robust cheering. Pretty fine organization, he thought. Maybe after law school and after he passed the bar…

He felt someone grab his arm. It was Lupe, and somehow he wound up behind her desk with the lady herself gazing up at him with a frown between her brows. "I want to ask you something."

"Ask away."

"You got the right intentions toward my girl, Detective?"

Taken aback, he whistled. "Um, we haven't talked about much of anything yet, Mrs. Delgado."

"Call me Lupe."

"Thank you, Lupe. And I'm Jackson."

Across the room, he could see Vanessa conversing with a couple of people he'd been introduced to but whose names he couldn't remember. She was dressed casually today, in black pants and a lightweight sweater the color of her eyes, all of which displayed her curves, right there for him to see and appreciate. And appreciate them he did.

She waved, he waved back.

Lupe tugged on his sleeve. "Pay attention here."

He redirected his gaze back to her. "Yes, ma'am."

"Don't mess with her, hear me? She's had enough trouble in her life."

Even though he knew the older woman had nothing but Vanessa's welfare at heart, he felt himself bristling. "I'm aware of that."

Now Lupe looked off in Vanessa's direction before turning back to Jackson, locking gazes with him, studying him, a fierce motherly protector. "I mean it."

"I'm not a bad man, Lupe," he told her.

She narrowed her gaze, then nodded. "That's what Mac says, but I needed to let you know how it is."

"I got it. You related on the mother or father's side?"

"Me? I'm no relation at all. My younger brother, Esteban, he was with her mom for a while, and I met Vanessa when she was a little older than Katy is now. Something about her got to me. I was never blessed with kids of my own, and she just filled in an empty spot. You know?"

He nodded. "I can imagine. She got to me, too. That's one special woman, that's for sure. And here she comes now."

Vanessa slipped her arm around Lupe's waist. "What kind of trash are you telling Jackson about me?"

"What makes you think we're talking about you?"

"The way both of you take occasional glances in my direction while your mouths form words," she said wryly. "It's kind of a giveaway."

"Lupe was just singing your praises," Jackson said. "And I was agreeing."

A becoming blush rose on her cheeks. "Now why'd you have to go and ruin my fun?"

"A compliment ruins your fun? Better get over that."

"Hey, Lupe," Mac called out from a few feet away.

"Wanda doesn't believe I take a walk every day while I'm here, just like the doc ordered. Come here and convince her."

Smiling, Lupe made her way through the crowd toward Mac and his wife. Vanessa turned to look at Jackson, suspicion in her eyes, which in this light were more green than blue. "Seriously, what did she say to you?"

"Nothing much, promise. Clucked a little about how I should be sure to treat you well. That kind of thing."

"I'm sorry."

"Why? Because someone loves you enough to care what happens to you?"

"Okay, I'm not sorry."

"Good. You and the kids doing anything next weekend?"

Vanessa, startled at his abrupt change of subject, did a double take. "Not really."

"Want to come out to my ranch?"

Okay, now she was really thrown. "Your what?"

"Well, it's not really a ranch," he said, scratching his head. "It's a couple of acres, is all. Way out past Simi Valley. I bought it as an investment about five years ago. One day I'll build a house on the property. It's zoned for horses and I plan on keeping a couple around. There's an old barn and a swing set. Come out next Sunday. Bring the kids."

Wow, she thought. A couple of acres. It sounded huge. She and her children had been surrounded by concrete most of their lives, with the occasional visit to a park or the beach. Where they lived now there were a few straggly trees. A couple of acres? A ranch? It sounded like heaven.

But…two hours today was one thing—was it okay for the whole family to spend an entire day with Jackson? Was it wise?

Before she could answer, Katy came running up to her, the other two and Lupe right behind her. "Mommy, Aunt Lupe says she has a new puppy. Can we go to her house?"

"I'll take them home after, Vanessa," Lupe said.

"You don't have to. I can pick them up."

"I said I'll take them home," the older woman said firmly. "Go off with Jackson. Have some fun."

He took her for a drive up Pacific Coast Highway, stopping at the bird sanctuary in Malibu. It was a small area consisting of a horseshoe-shaped beach nestled between the ocean and a saltwater creek, hidden from the main highway. After Jackson spread out a blanket on the sand, they sat side by side, staring at the antics of gulls, pigeons, herons, pelicans, ducks, terns. Watched them fly off in flocks, swoop down again, gather in clumps, chatter like neighbors over a back fence.

It was a beautiful day; the air smelled of salt and kelp. Vanessa took it all in, feeling light and young inside. She shook her head in wonder. "I had no idea this was here."

"Found it by accident. Birds are somethin' else, aren't they? I'll probably turn into one of those old geezers with a white beard and binoculars around his neck."

Wasn't that interesting, she thought. She'd also always found birds fascinating. "Have you ever seen a movie called *The Wild Parrots of Telegraph Hill?*"

"No."

"It's amazing. It's about this hippie guy up in San Francisco that develops a kind of family with all these parrots. In the beginning they all look alike, then you start to see the differences, start to care about them as individuals. When one of them died I cried."

"Softy, huh?"

As though it were the most natural thing in the world, he put his arm around her and she rested against his shoulder, feeling small and protected and very, very safe. It was not a familiar feeling…and it was lovely. Together they sat and watched the birds and talked of light, inconsequential things. When Jackson asked her to have dinner with him, she used his cell phone to call over to Lupe's and make sure Shane would get Katy to bed once they got home, and would lock both doors and let no one in, no matter what.

They headed back toward the city, stopping off at a fish place on the way. It was noisy, filled with a young, boisterous crowd, so conversation was difficult. Both were pleased to return to the quiet of Jackson's car.

Instead of taking the ramp up to Ocean Avenue, Jackson stayed on the coast road as it narrowed, pulling off onto a tree-shrouded, twisting dirt path. They climbed upward for a couple of minutes until they reached a flat plateau that looked out onto Pacific Coast Highway and the ocean beyond.

He stopped the car, turned off the engine and the lights. The moon was a sliver in the distance. There was no one around them, no people, no other cars. The dark night enveloped Vanessa like a whisper-soft blanket. "You know all kinds of secret places, don't you," she whispered—somehow a whisper was called for up here.

"I like to explore." He put his arm around her, drew her close, nuzzled her ear. "Right now I'd like to explore you."

The kiss began softly, to go with the quiet of the night. But it didn't stay that way. In no time at all, Jackson's mouth was doing its magic, sucking her tongue into his, then planting more kisses all over her face, her neck, along her collarbones. She responded instantly. Her blood surged wildly through her system, heat throbbed in the pit of her stomach and between her legs. He pulled the scoop neck of her sweater down and nibbled along the top of her breast. When his hand cupped the underside of one, his thumb flicking at her nipple, it took all the effort she could muster to push his hand away and sit back, barely able to catch her breath.

"No," she managed to get out. "I can't."

"I won't hurt you."

"No, it's not that." She forced herself to face him, gulped in another quick breath before saying, "It's been a very long time. Years."

His shadowed gaze was intense. "Since what, exactly?"

"Since I've been with a man. And I don't think I've ever enjoyed sex," she added, amazed at how she'd just blurted out something she barely admitted to herself. She hadn't planned this, not at all. "I mean, sex that was for me, not for—" she raised a shoulder, lowered it "—not for pay."

It was his turn to suck in a breath. Then he blew it out, nodded. "Okay," he said slowly. "Got it. First-time jitters."

"Um, not exactly my first time."

"Your first time with me, yeah it is." One side of his mouth quirked up. "And in case you're thinking you're frigid, allow me to disagree."

"You don't know that."

"Yeah, I do." He put his arm around her again, drew her close. "You don't have to be scared, darlin'. We won't do much. Not tonight."

"But—"

He covered her mouth with a kiss, murmuring, "I want to give you pleasure, nothing more."

"We're in public," she said, her will weakening.

"No one can see." Again he nuzzled her neck. Again her nipples hardened immediately, and a sharp ache between her legs was followed by the release of moisture. She had no more resistance left in her. Not with all the weapons Jackson used. His mouth, his tongue, his fingers. His touch was magical. All he had to do was reach under her sweater, push her bra up, tongue her nipple, and she nearly jumped out of her seat.

So this was what passion was, she realized through a fog of red-hot sensations. *Real* passion, not manufactured for the customer, or not driven by the fear that she'd be beaten.

The world was spinning. She felt his hand pulling her pants partway down so he could reach between her legs. For a moment she stiffened.

"I'd never do anything to hurt you, Vanessa," he said softly, stroking her. "See? Just this, nothing more."

His tongue traced her ear while his fingers found the tight knot of nerves between her thighs and worked it, slowly, sensually. She felt more moisture down there, felt her hips moving, felt herself climbing, heard herself moaning, knew she was losing herself and didn't mind at all.

"Take your time, darlin'," Jackson whispered.

"I...don't think I can." She could barely get it out, she was gasping so hard, the sound going out into the dark, velvety night. Faster and faster he rubbed and higher and higher she climbed. Until suddenly her world exploded. He caught her mouth on a long scream of completion, stayed with her and caught her as she fell.

On Thursday morning, as Vanessa and Katy headed for the carport, Ray sauntered up to them. "Hey, *chica.*"

She clutched Katy's hand tightly, looked around her quickly to see if there were any neighbors who might help. No one. Just her and Katy and Ray. She held her daughter tightly against her leg and said nothing.

Ray moved closer, put his hand on her shoulder. "I said hey, 'Nessa."

She shook off his hand, forcing herself to look into his flat, hard eyes. She was quaking inside. Would she ever stop quaking in the presence of this man? This devil?

She remembered what she'd been taught: It didn't matter what she was feeling inside, only how she appeared on the outside. "I heard you," she said briskly. "I have to get to work."

Ignoring her, Ray got down on his haunches, facing Katy, who clung to Vanessa's skirt. "Hey, Katy."

Her little girl's grip on her mother's leg grew tighter.

"Hey, Katy," he said again, using that purring, seductive voice of his. "Know who I am?"

"Ray," Vanessa warned.

"I'm your daddy. Did you know you have a daddy? Did your mama tell you?"

Katy, still clinging hard, gazed up at her, huge dark-brown eyes—Ray's eyes—filled with doubt. "Mom?"

She shook her head. "Say goodbye, Katy. We have to get you to school."

She tried to walk, but Ray stood and got in her face. "So, you didn't tell Katy about me, huh? Didn't even give her a chance to get to know her daddy?"

"I owe you nothing, Ray." She hated how her voice was quivering.

Again his eyes turned flat and cold. "Listen, *chica.* You really don't want to mess with me."

The sound of the back door to their apartment drew her gaze away from Ray. Both boys came out, walking stiffly, all brave fronts, a little fear in their eyes.

"Mom?" Shane said. "You okay here?"

Ray looked over, assessed them in one quick glance and smiled. "Hey, Shane? Thomas? How you doing?"

They looked at him, then at their mother one more time. Thomas swallowed, then said, "Mom?"

Ray swaggered over. "You look good, boys. Turned out just fine." He put up his hand for a high-five, but both kept their hands at their sides.

Vanessa could see from his posture that Ray didn't like being dissed, not in the least. "Boys," she said, "Ray was just leaving. We all have to get ready for school."

Ray stood his ground, still facing her sons. "You two know who I am, right? I mean that I'm Katy's daddy. And I'm the one who sent you those presents. The Game

Boy, the Xbox?" He angled his body so all of them were in his sight. "And, Katy, I was the one sent you the Barbie dolls, and the pretty dresses. The ones your mom made you give back?"

Both boys looked at her, not sure what to do next. Katy too remained mute. The surge of hate Vanessa felt toward Ray at that moment, for trying to play with her kids' heads, gave her momentary strength.

"Please leave them alone," Vanessa said sharply. "Leave all my children alone. Boys, go back into the apartment. You have a school bus to catch in ten minutes."

Both stood their ground, stubborn looks on their faces. Shane crossed his arms over his chest, as if to say that until his mom was okay, he wasn't going anywhere. Her heart ached with love for him, even as her fear for Ray's unpredictability grew.

At that moment, another neighbor came out of his apartment, heading toward his car, whistling. Mr. Otunabe was a recent immigrant from Nigeria, who practiced his English with the family whenever he could. "Good day to you, Mrs. Garner," he said in his beautiful, lilting voice, a sunny smile lighting up his ebony face. "And to Katy and Shane and Thomas. Isn't the day a fine one?"

"Yes, it is, Mr. Otunabe," Vanessa said with a relieved smile. "And if my boys don't get into the house now, and make sure the door is locked behind them, the day will be a lot less fine," she said pointedly. "Come, Katy. We need to get going."

Mr. Otunabe seemed to pick up on the tension then, and he stood, puzzled, gazing from Vanessa to the boys to Ray, not quite sure what to do.

Ray did not always act like a sane man, but he chose that moment to use his brain. If he had planned to harm any of them, there were too many witnesses. *Thank you, Mr. Otunabe,* Vanessa said silently.

Ray shot her another look that said they weren't done yet, and slowly sauntered off, turning down the alleyway that led to the street. After a moment Shane took off after him.

"Shane," Vanessa called out in alarm.

He put a hand up and said quietly, "I'll be cool, Mom. Just making sure." And before she could protest further, he'd disappeared around the corner.

Mr. Otunabe frowned. "You are okay, Mrs. Garner?"

"I'm not sure." Heart in her throat, she kept her gaze on the spot where she'd last seen Shane.

In a few moments he came sprinting back, nodding. "He's gone."

She exhaled a relieved breath. "I'm okay now, Mr. Otunabe, thank you for asking."

"You are sure?"

She smiled at him. "Yes. Please, don't let me keep you."

He gave a tentative smile, then walked down the alleyway to his car.

After he was out of earshot, Vanessa turned to her sons. "And thank you, Shane and Thomas, for—" she had to swallow down some strong emotion before continuing "—defending me like that. Promise me, if ever you see that man again, run the other way, you hear me?"

"Is he really Katy's dad?" Thomas asked.

"Biologically, yes," she said, looking from him to his

older brother, who had an unreadable expression on his face. "Tonight," she added. "Tonight I'll sit you down and explain the whole thing. I should have done it before. Now get going. And be sure to watch out for Ray. If you didn't get it before, you get it now. He's bad news. Really bad news. Got me?"

She waited until they nodded. "Okay, Mom," Shane said.

"Got it," Thomas said.

They turned and went back into the house. Her heart was filled with so much pride and love she thought it might burst. Quickly she took Katy's hand and headed for her car.

They were halfway to Katy's school before her little girl spoke up. "I have a daddy?"

"Everyone has a daddy, honey."

"The bad man is my daddy?"

"Yes, he is."

"Why is he a bad man?"

She'd always wondered how she would answer these questions, and now the time was here. "A long time ago, before you were born, he was very nasty to me."

"Did he yell at you?"

"Yes. And he hit me. And it hurt. A lot."

Katy frowned. "That's not nice."

"No it's not. *He's* not nice, honey."

Vanessa took a quick glance at her child's face, which wore an expression that said she was trying to figure all this out. Then she burst into tears. "My daddy is a bad man."

She reached over, stroked Katy's head, thinking

wildly, I have no idea how to explain this, what words to say. "Don't think of him as your daddy, honey. All he did was plant the seed."

This, they had talked about. How fathers planted seeds and mothers made them grow. At six, Katy seemed okay with that concept of where babies came from, even if she did ask once why, if there were seeds involved, she didn't have leaves.

Katy's tears didn't last long; they rarely did. And for a while longer there was silence in the car. Vanessa had just begun to breathe a sigh of relief when the little girl popped up with, "Is the bad man Shane and Thomas's daddy, too?"

"No, honey. They have different daddies."

"Where are they?"

"I don't know."

A semi-lie. One was dead from an overdose, the other had taken off long before Vanessa had known she was pregnant and she hadn't bothered to find him in the years since. Perhaps she needed to do just that, just in case. Just to be prepared.

She shook her head. Her old life. She kept trying to start over, the way Jackson's seven-year theory went. Instead her past came back to haunt her every time.

This time she knew not to expect Katy's silence to last. Sure enough, here came another. "I know he's bad, but didn't he want to be with us?"

"I didn't want to be with him."

"But—"

"Katy, honey, I wish I could explain it better, but sometimes you just have to trust Mommy. He's not a good person and I don't want him near you. I promise when you're older I'll explain it better. Okay?"

She got that look on her face, the one with the twisted little mouth, that said she hated her mother's "when you're older" answer, one she'd heard before. Then she crossed her arms over her small chest and pouted.

Vanessa sighed. She had to find the right words. There must be the right words out there. Somewhere.

"Hi," Jackson said in a soft voice.

"Hi, back," she replied into the receiver, snuggling a little deeper under the covers. He'd called every night this week at bedtime. It had become the highlight of her day.

"Anyone ever tell you that you have the sexiest voice in the world?"

"Someone just did. How was work today?"

"Too much paperwork, too much bad coffee, trying to get this wave of bad guys off the street before the next wave comes along. You know, the usual. And yours?"

She hesitated. She needed to tell him about the encounter with Ray this morning, but there was a part of her that feared his reaction. Jackson kept a tight rein on his anger, but it was there, underneath, and she'd always been uncomfortable around angry men. She'd known too many of them.

Still, she knew what she had to do. "Ray came by this morning."

"What?" His tone lost all traces of easy conversation. "Why didn't you call me right away? Did he threaten you? Harm you in any way?"

Waves of fury came over the phone line and she had

to take in a deep breath, reminding herself that it wasn't directed at her, but on her behalf. "I'm fine, Jackson. Promise."

She waited, gave him time to calm down. Then he said, "Okay, tell me what happened." She did so, leaving nothing out. When she was done, he said, "You need to take out a restraining order."

Her laugh was bitter. "Yeah, right. I tried that once. It didn't work."

"What happened?"

"One of his cops—he had a couple on the payroll— told him about it before he was even served. He found me and nearly killed me. I was carrying Katy at the time, and I spent the rest of the pregnancy in fear that he'd damaged her, too."

After several muttered curses, Jackson asked, "Did you file charges?"

"His last words to me were that if I told anyone who had done this to me, he'd kill my kids. And I believed him. So the answer is no, I didn't."

She heard a loud pounding as though he'd punched his fist into something solid. "Jackson?"

"If I weren't on the job," he said with more intensity than she'd ever heard from him, "I'd pay him a visit. In fact I might pay him a visit anyway. He's not done, Vanessa."

"I know."

She waited, knew he was mulling something over. Funny how in the short time they'd known each other, she was able to sense him and his moods, even over the phone.

On the other end of the line, Jackson was shaking his

left hand to get some feeling back into it. Classic stupid move, to punch a hard wooden table—the table always won. But damn, this Ray Ortiz had to be dealt with. He'd never felt like murdering someone in cold blood before, but it was up for him now. The man was a violent dirt bag, and the world would be better off without him.

Great fantasy, Rutherford. Now on to reality. "Look, let me think up a few ways to deal with this okay? Meantime, get a cell phone. I'll pay for it if you can't afford it."

"Jackson, I—"

"Don't fight me on this, Vanessa. This is for your protection, for your kids. It's an emergency. Do it. And put my numbers, my home, my office and my cell in speed dial. The minute you see him, you hear from him, *anything,* you call me. Got it?"

She didn't reply for a while and he wondered if he'd come down on her too hard. She didn't appreciate being given orders or giving control to others—he knew that about her. But he'd do it again, if it meant keeping her alive.

Finally she admitted, "You're right. I keep hoping he'll go away, but that's burying my head in the sand. I'll get a cell phone tomorrow." She gave a rueful chuckle. "Shane will be thrilled. That will mean he can talk to whatever girlfriend he has that week for hours and I can't complain."

"You got great kids. They took care of you today. Let me take care of you, too."

There was another long silence before she said softly, "You have no idea what that means to me. Thank you, Jackson. Good night."

"Good night."

He hung up the phone, his chest churning with all kinds of emotions. Fear for her, worry about what Ray would do next. Respect for her strength of character. Even something approaching—

Uh-oh. Love?

No, he told himself. Not possible. Too soon. They hadn't even slept together yet. And hadn't he made a mental note a few days ago to give major thought to their relationship? To their being a "couple"? Then what was he doing, calling her night after night? Telling her she had a sexy voice? What was he doing, flexing his muscles, getting all Me-Tarzan-you-Jane protective, telling her he'd take care of the bad guy and take care of her, too? This was nuts! When had Vanessa crept into his head and heart with so much impact as to block out all the impediments to their being together? When had she taken over?

And what was he going to do about it?

Too wired to sleep, he decided to take a long drive. The night was clear and dark as he drove north on Lincoln. When the sign for the freeway loomed ahead, he swung onto the ramp. He knew just where to go. He'd done some background checking on Ray Ortiz and had his address. Jackson had one of those memories that saw something once and remembered it, so he headed into the Valley.

Ray and his wife lived in Encino, of all places, way far removed from the San Diego barrio where he'd grown up and the streets of Montebello where he'd established his street creds in the violent world of crack and heroin. Encino was upper-middle-class suburbia, filled with lawyers and doctors, successful business owners. Ray going for some respect, a little fitting in to the American Dream. Jackson wondered if his neighbors knew anything about his little occupation. Did Ray and Sharon Ortiz throw parties? Did they grill steaks on the barbecue for other families on the block, discuss stock options while the man of the house wore a big apron and chef's hat?

He found the address, on a street filled with large homes representing a cross section of styles—Mission adobe, Nantucket clapboard, brick Colonial. Ray's was a big sucker, kind of a faux Southern plantation with thick white columns on a porch that ran the full width of the place. The lawn was manicured, the shrubs well-tended. There was money behind this, and Jackson had a feeling that it was not just drug money but Sharon's family money that had contributed.

A couple of upper-story lights were on, and for a moment he sat in his car and pondered paying the man a little visit. The thought of it got his blood going, and he realized he wouldn't be able to keep it civil. He was always able to contain his rage…except when it came to protecting Vanessa.

Which meant if he saw Ray tonight, he would hit him. Probably more than once. And probably way too hard. Which would be fine if there were no witnesses, but Ray had a wife, so it wasn't a good idea.

Okay then, he decided, not now, not tonight.

But the day would come. Whatever happened between Jackson and Vanessa—whether they wound up together or as a pleasant memory to be taken out and visited once in a while—there would be a reckoning between him and Ray Ortiz.

Count on it.

Chapter 6

The next night, even over the phone line, Jackson's chuckle warmed her. "Katy did what?"

"Told her teacher that she didn't want to be a daisy in the school play, because it was too common, that she preferred to be an 'amarlilly.' When I asked her if she meant an amaryllis or a lily, she insisted I show her pictures of both and decided on an amaryllis, because it was 'exonic' and when she grew up she was going to be really 'exonic.'"

"She's got her mom's love of words, for sure."

"And one of these days she'll get them right."

He chuckled again. A comfortable silence went by before Jackson, his voice lowering to an intimate growl, said, "Want to know what I'm thinking about right now?"

Vanessa pulled the covers up around her neck—it

was still chilly at night, even in May—and said, "I'm not sure. Do I?"

"You. The way you were with me on Sunday. You remember."

She felt a warning shiver go through her body. Something deep inside her was disturbed by the turn the conversation had taken. "This is so weird."

"What is?"

She shook her head. "I just had a flashback. Sorry."

"Tell me."

"You don't want to know."

"Yeah, I do," he replied.

Except for last night's discussion about Ray, all their talks this week had been mostly how-was-your-day? topics. As though by mutual agreement, they'd both realized they needed to take it slow, get to know each other. She hadn't expected tonight's exchange to turn either sensual or serious, but it had. And she knew she owed him the truth about herself; with all the generosity he'd displayed toward her and her kids, he'd earned it.

"Okay, here's what the flashback was about," she began. "For a long time I thought about my body as…well, as a commodity. Men used to pay me for its use, Jackson. I learned tricks to please them. I learned how to use my body to get money, but I always kept my mind separate. I was raped, I was beaten, I was rented out, and all because men wanted my body. Not me, never me. My body. So talking about sex, it's…not something I'm used to. Or comfortable with. I can't laugh about it."

He let a beat go by before saying, "I got you. But

you've changed, right? You're not the same person you were back then, are you?"

"No, of course I'm not."

"When we kiss, when I kiss you, is it uncomfortable?"

She released a large sigh. "Far from it," she admitted.

"The other day," he murmured, "when I had my hand between your legs and you moaned and shuddered, did you find that uncomfortable?"

A surge of heat shot through her, despite her memories. "You don't play fair. I'm trying to tell you—" She paused, not sure just what she wanted to tell him.

"What?"

"What happened, it's all part of me, Jackson. Back then I was so lost, a junkie who needed her next fix—" Again she stopped, unable to bear the wave of emotion that swept over her.

"You forgiven yourself for that yet, Vanessa?" he asked softly.

"I thought I had. Now I'm not so sure."

"Oh, darlin'. All I can say is, that was then. A long time ago."

She managed a small smile. "Your seven-year theory. I know. But, I think, by nature, you're more of an optimist than I am. I still get these dark pictures in my head."

A beat went by before Jackson said, "We all have pictures, Vanessa."

"You too?"

"I saw men blown up in battle and I couldn't save them. My little brother drowned when I was eight and I couldn't save him. My daddy was in pain for three years before he died, and he kept refusing medication because he didn't want to look weak. Can you believe that? He was terminal, he knew it, but he was afraid of being thought of as unmanly. I can still see him, his wasted body, his white face, trying not to cry out with the pain." His voice broke on the last few words and her heart hurt for him.

"Oh, Jackson."

She heard him swallow before saying, "So, yeah, I got some pictures of my own."

Shame filled her. She'd been self-centered, so involved in her own dark memories she hadn't even considered his. "I'm so sorry."

He wasn't done. "And yeah, I'm a guy. A big guy, so no, I've never been abused. Beaten. Raped. So I don't know how that feels. And, yeah, it sucks. Big-time. But it's not a reason to stop living."

"I live," she said, strong and on the defensive.

"Only with part of you. The other part—the life force? The sexual part of you? That's been shut down for a long time. You need to give yourself a chance to be a woman again."

"And you'll be only too happy to help me, right?" she countered sarcastically.

"If you think all I see when I look at you is a body," Jackson retorted with what she could tell was a mixture of hurt and anger, "if you think I'm like all the johns in your past— Hell, if you think I don't know there's a real-life, flesh and blood, complex woman in there, then you don't know me at all."

His outburst effectively shut down the conversation for the moment. Oh, God, Vanessa thought, she'd done it again, lumped him in with all "men." And she'd wounded him in the process. "I'm sorry," she said finally. "I didn't mean it the way it came out. I know you're not like the men in my past, but...well, I'm really sorry."

"Yeah, well, me too. Kind of hit a sore spot there." She heard him take in a breath and expel it. "But, please, help me here. Tell me what I can do. Tell me what you're afraid of."

Oh, boy. Down-and-dirty truth time. "I'm afraid of not being good enough," she admitted. "Of disappointing you. Or being *too* good, too practiced. I've never had anything remotely *normal* with a man before. I'm afraid I won't know how to just react, to just *be*."

"Oh, darlin'," he said, all traces of irritation with her gone, replaced by a smile in his voice. "All of us are afraid, sometimes. Been afraid too many times to count, myself."

"You? Not possible," she said, only partly kidding.

"Possible," he said. "Trust me. And with that, I'll say good night. See you Sunday at ten."

They sat side by side, leaning against the trunk of an old oak tree on his property. The kids were running around as if they'd been cooped up inside for days. They'd already explored the barn, the softball equipment. Katy had discovered the old swing set, which made a god-awful sound but still functioned. At the moment Jackson and Vanessa were watching while Shane pushed Katy on the swing and Thomas kicked a soccer ball around.

"Look at them," Vanessa said with a smile. "So young. So much energy."

"Yeah," Jackson agreed, but his mind was trying to sort out a whole bunch of stuff.

Like the fact that he'd never brought a woman to his property before, not to mention a woman with kids.

Like the fact that the only times he'd talked about his experiences in the Marines, his brother's drowning, his father's last days, were in passing. Tossed off. Historical info, when necessary.

He'd never gotten into the really intimate stuff about himself with anyone before, man or woman, and yet here he was, allowing Vanessa and her kids to invade his private space, allowing Vanessa herself to invade his private hell. No, not allowing her to invade—more like offering himself up to her, inviting her in.

It made him uncomfortable as hell. All of this was more than he'd bargained for. What was the word the touchy-feely shrinks used on talk radio? Vulnerable. Yeah, he was finding himself vulnerable to Vanessa, and he wasn't sure just how he'd gotten here. Hell, they hadn't even slept together yet and he was letting her see his guts, talking to her about really private things.

And she was doing the same with him. He knew that what they'd talked about the other night on the phone wasn't stuff she shared easily, either. If at all.

He turned to look at her, watching her profile as she feasted on the sight of her city-bound kids experiencing real country-style freedom. In the shade of the huge old oak, her skin took on a dusky golden hue.

"That little talk we had a couple of nights ago," he found himself saying. "You okay with it?"

She turned and smiled at him, those astonishing blue-green eyes wide and clear and totally lacking in guile. "Mostly. You?"

He shrugged. "Yeah, I guess."

"You do push," she said, "but I guess, sometimes, I need some pushing."

"Let me know if it's too much."

"Oh, I will, trust me," she said, with another smile, before turning back to watch the kids again.

Vulnerable. The word came back to him. He was having some pretty powerful feelings about this woman. Yeah, he still wanted her—and would have her—but there were all these other emotions, ones he hadn't experienced before. If you were vulnerable to someone that meant they could hurt you. Vanessa could hurt him, and deeply, a position he'd never found himself in with other women. She was becoming a part of his life and he hadn't even yet decided—in his head—if that was a good idea. The thing was, his head wasn't involved in this one.

He'd even told Mama about her, last week and just the other night on the phone. Casually, of course, no big deal. That he was dating someone, nothing much. But Mama, who knew her boy pretty well, had started darting questions at him. She wanted details, and he'd given her some but had been pretty stingy with them. There would be more and more questions to come. He needed to know the answers to some of them himself.

But for now his head hurt.

He went back to relaxing against the tree, enjoying the breeze, the sounds of birds chirping, the sight of children at play.

* * *

When Jackson took her hand in his, Vanessa gazed at him for a moment, and wondered how she had gotten so lucky. She'd done so many wrong things in her life. What had she done right to deserve this kind, patient man? And, yes, she was aware that both of them were in that heart-fluttering, beginning-of-the-relationship cloud. And, yes, she knew there would have to be a reality check somewhere down the road and that they either would or would not survive that—most likely not.

But couldn't she just enjoy this precious time out of time, this sensation of being pretty and feminine, cherished and desired, even respected, by a good, strong man, even if it eventually went nowhere?

Who would she hurt if she indulged herself, just this once. No one but herself, and she'd survived an awful lot of pain already. Whatever life threw at her, as the old feminist anthem went, she would survive.

Then he let the bombshell drop. "Oh, by the way," he said, tossing it off casually, "my mama's coming out for a visit."

"Oh?"

"Yeah. I been telling her about you. She wants to meet you."

One reality check, coming right up.

Vanessa shot him a startled look. "She what?"

"Wants to see this woman who's been taking up so much room in my head."

"How could you?"

"How could I what?"

"Do that? Tell her about me? I mean it's so soon. We barely know each other."

"Actually, we do," he said thoughtfully. "In all the important ways. The rest is details, your stories, my stories. Lots of time for that."

She wasn't ready to be mollified. "Jackson, I mean it. She'll think we're serious."

"Are we?"

Again, his question took her by surprise. She threw up her hands. "It's too soon. I don't know. What do you think?"

He frowned, then shrugged. "Yeah, it's early days yet. But look, darlin', just tell yourself you're meeting someone's mama and leave it at that. Not a biggie."

"Easy for you to say."

"Not really, but—" again he shrugged "—Mama's coming anyway."

A frown formed between her brows. "When?"

"In the next week or so. She's visiting an old school friend in Arizona right now. She'll let me know."

"So soon? Oh, God. Does she know I have kids?"

"Sure does."

"Does she know I'm not the same race as you?"

The truth was, Jackson hadn't yet decided if he should or shouldn't mention race to his mama. There were arguments to be made on both sides.

Or maybe he was a coward.

"What is your ethnic background, by the way?" he said. "I've been meaning to ask you."

"You're changing the subject."

"Only partially."

She glared at him for a moment, but he remained silent. Then she shrugged. "I don't know exactly. My mother's gone now, but she was mostly Latina and Filipino, and she *thought,* although she wasn't sure, that one set of grandparents were Lithuanian Jews. She also thought my father was one half Vietnamese and the other half black—a byproduct of the Vietnam war. But, as you may have guessed, she wasn't sure."

"Bunch of choices there."

"Just a few," she agreed wryly. "I'm classically multi-racial. Not one thing or another. Like Tiger Woods. Did you know that he's one quarter African-American, one quarter Thai, one quarter Chinese, one eighth American Indian and one eighth Caucasian?"

He plum loved the way Vanessa's face took on a live-liness when she was discussing topics of interest to her. She'd been born to soak up knowledge. "I had no idea. Old Tiger is a one-man melting pot."

"Except that the melting pot image isn't in favor at the moment. I took a class a couple of years ago on the racial and ethnic strains in the American population—'multi-cultural studies' they called it. To multiculturists, the melting pot image means losing all other identities, you know, becoming like the dominant ingredient—having to choose sides. They prefer the concept of *ajiaco,* which is Spanish for stew. Lots of things mixed together, but not so you can't taste the individual flavors."

"I had no idea about all this," he said. He would need to do some studying up on the subject himself. "I'm curious, though. Do you identify more with one race than the others?"

The look she gave him was sharp and just a tad leery. "Would it matter?"

He shrugged, aware that they were finally touching on a topic that needed discussion. "I honestly don't think so. Race isn't that big a deal to me. But if it popped up, we would talk about it."

He could see her wariness lessen, which meant he'd at least not given the wrong answer. Whew.

"If I had to choose," she said thoughtfully, "and I don't, I guess Lupe's influence, the Hispanic culture— the cooking, the expressions, you know, all of that—is the strongest. But mostly I figure I'm an American and try to leave it at that. I tell that to the kids, too. And by the way, unlike my mother, I *do* know who all their fathers were—I was living with each of them at the time. But except for Ray, whose people were from Guatemala, I'm not sure about their racial makeup."

Ray. Jackson didn't want to think about the man, because every time he did, his temper got going and that took his mind off other things. Like how he really loved to study Vanessa, her striking face, the strong bones, the sensual mouth. Not for the first time something in his chest flipped over. Her honesty, her strength of character, together with her looks, well, the woman simply took his breath away.

Were they "serious"? Were they a "couple?" Did he have to know now, right this moment?

He reached up and stroked her cheek, then took her hand in his again. "It can't be easy for you, and it won't be easy for the kids. But lots of things in life aren't easy. On a lighter note, may I say that whoever and whatever your ancestors were, they created one hell of an exotic, sexy, *beautiful* woman."

Her eyes widened with surprise at his change of subject, then she cast them down, obviously pleased but just a little embarrassed. "You know just the right thing to say, don't you?"

"We aim to please, ma'am," he responded with a grin.

At that moment Thomas came running up to them. "Hey, Jackson. Wanna throw the ball around?"

"Looks like I'm being summoned." He got up, brushed off the back of his jeans and said to Vanessa, "We'll work it all out."

"But there's so very much of it to work out."

"Hey, no pain, no gain, right?"

For the next half hour the men played ball and Vanessa stayed near Katy while the little girl attempted to "reach the sky" on the swing. It was a beautiful spring day in Southern California, not too hot yet. Fluffy white clouds raced across sky the color of Jackson's eyes. As she watched her children and the man in her life interacting with ease, it was deeply tempting to imagine it could be like this. That a family with a father, mother and three kids was possible, that all the issues between Jackson and her could be, as he had said, "dealt with." Oh, so tempting.

Tempting, too, was the thought that she could have anything approaching a healthy sexual relationship with a lover. How did he feel about that part of her history? Most men wouldn't be able to get past the fact that she'd sold her body. Was it possible that Jackson was one of the exceptions?

And then there were her kids, who had been looking at him all day, even Shane, with something close to hero worship. They were starved for a male figure in their lives. Would that be Jackson? And if it didn't work out, just how heartbroken would they be?

Were any of her dreams even remotely possible in the real world? In the real world where Jackson's old-fashioned, Southern born and bred mama would soon be paying a visit?

Had she made a mistake letting him so thoroughly into their lives? Would there be pain and a sense of abandonment down the road when the real world began to interfere?

Or was she, as he'd said earlier, using fear to keep herself from growing, from taking chances, from living a full and complete life? Again, she had no answers. None at all.

Vanessa stood in the grocery store aisle, reading the label of the new cereal Thomas wanted her to get, but it seemed to her that its number one ingredient was sugar. Gee what a surprise, she thought, wryly amused. Her own little sugar addict with his round face and sweet smile.

"Vanessa?"

Startled by a voice over her left shoulder, she turned to see a woman gazing at her with a hesitant smile on her face. She was about her own age and had the faded-blond prettiness usually associated with older women. Her hair was thin and worn shoulder length, and she was dressed in a beautifully cut beige pantsuit with a cream shell. She wore large diamond studs in her ears and sported another generous diamond and matching wedding band on her ring finger. The most striking feature though were her eyes—large and pale gray, and sad.

So sad, it was as though someone had died.

"Excuse me?"

"You're Vanessa Garner, aren't you?"

"Do I know you?"

The woman shot her another small, tentative smile. "No, no, of course you don't." She held out her hand. "I'm Sharon. Sharon Ortiz."

Vanessa, who had been about to shake the woman's hand, let hers drop to her side without completing the gesture. "Ray's wife?"

"Yes."

Vanessa looked around her. "Where is he?"

"Who?"

"Ray. He must be here somewhere."

She shook her head. "No. He doesn't even know I'm here."

"Right."

"I mean that. I don't think he'd like it if he knew about it."

As she studied the other woman for a moment, Vanessa had a feeling she was lying; on the other hand, Ray's wife had one of those faces that always looked as though she were lying. A kind of apologetic, hangdog expression. "How did you find me?"

"I'm sorry. I followed you, from your house."

Not pleased at being stalked, Vanessa pushed her cart away. "I have nothing to say to you."

Sharon followed her. "Please, please, won't you talk to me just for minute?"

"I really don't think it would do any good."

"We could go somewhere? Have a cup of coffee?"

She shook her head, kept walking. "Sorry, no. I don't have time."

They were now at the rear of the market in the meat section. Vanessa studied the selection, trying to find something discounted but not too near the expiration date and wishing Sharon would go away. Was she being unreasonable? she wondered. Punishing a woman because she'd made the unfortunate mistake of marrying a monster? Sharon didn't seem to be a bad person. Weak. Sad. Filled with shame. But not evil.

The blond woman looked around to see if anyone was nearby, then grasped the edge of the cart and said softly, "I don't know if Ray told you or not, but I have…fertility problems."

"Yes, he mentioned it."

"Do you have any idea how that feels?"

She shook her head. "No, I'm sorry I don't."

"Do you have any idea how hard it is to live with that? When all you want, when all you've ever wanted, was to be a mother, to hold your tiny little baby in your arms and bury your nose in its soft neck? The tests, the monthly waiting, the, well, the obsession. You can't think of anything else, can't do anything else." Sharon's pale eyes filled with tears. "All you can think about is the baby you want, you *need,* and it about drives you crazy."

"I'm sorry," Vanessa said and she meant it. All the misery on the woman's face made her grateful that, whatever pain and sadness she'd had in her life, that particular experience hadn't been hers. Quite the opposite, in fact, she thought with irony, although it would be cruel of her to mention that.

A couple of other shoppers wheeled their carts by, and Sharon's gaze darted from left to right as she swiped the edge of her hand under her eyelids. Seeming to gather herself, she said quietly, "Ray and I, well, we really want a child."

"Why not adopt?"

Sharon shook her head. "Ray…doesn't like that suggestion."

No, Vanessa thought. Of course not. Adopting wouldn't go along with his "king of the macho warriors" self-image.

"And, well, I was wondering," Sharon went on. "I thought maybe, you know, if you met me and saw that I'm a good person and that I'll make a good mother and that Katy would get all the best in life, that maybe you would, you know—" She left the sentence incomplete.

This was incredible, absolutely incredible. Did the woman have any idea what she was asking? "You thought I would let her go? That my heart would soften for your plight?"

Sharon gave a little shrug. "I hoped, yes."

Sighing, Vanessa said, "I'm sorry you can't have a child, but if you had one, you would know not only how impossible it would be to let her go to someone else, but how unthinkable the entire suggestion is."

The tears were back; Sharon's entire thin body sagged against the meat counter. Vanessa couldn't help the stab of guilt for her bounty when this woman had none. But she brushed it away. This was not her problem. Ray, his wife, all of it was not her problem and she needed to remember that. "I'm sorry. I wish there were something I could do."

"There is." She grabbed Vanessa by the upper arm; her grip was surprisingly strong. The look in her eyes was desperate. Her gaze darted about the market wildly, as though afraid, then it returned to meet Vanessa's eyes again. "I have to— I mean, *please.*"

She got it then, and she wrenched her arm away from Sharon's grip, disgusted with herself. "He *did* send you, didn't he? He told you that you had a chance if you talked to me."

"He said that it was up to me. That you have a soft spot."

"I do," she said grimly, "but not when it comes to my kids and someone trying to take one of them away."

The woman twisted her hands together nervously. "He'll be so angry."

Shaking her head, she studied her. "How often does he beat you?"

"What? Oh, no. He doesn't lay a hand on me. Of course not."

Of course yes, Vanessa said silently, but kept it to herself. The woman was fragile, barely holding on to her sanity and not only because of her infertility. Abused women always lied to others and to themselves. If they were lucky, they woke up one day and stopped lying. If they weren't, they often wound up on a slab in the morgue. For Sharon Ortiz's sake, she hoped that would not be her path.

"Is he waiting for you outside?"

Sharon looked down at her feet, shook her head in a gesture of hopelessness. "No. He's…away for a couple of days. On business."

Vanessa gazed at the woman's sad, defeated posture and felt another twist of pity for her. There, but for the grace of, etcetera, she thought. "Look, I really do have to go. I wish you luck."

She pushed her cart down a nearby aisle, then paused for a moment to look back. Sharon Ortiz stood just where she'd left her, dejected, her shoulders slumped, staring sightlessly at something on the ground. For all her "family money" and the pretty all-American looks, she could have posed for a painting entitled Portrait of Despair.

When Jackson and Sal got back to their desks, they looked at each other and raised their right hands for a huge high-five. "Yes!" Sal said, his classically Italian features with their down-turned brown eyes and generous nose transformed into a grinning happy face. "We got the suckers!"

"One for the good guys," Jackson agreed, feeling pretty good himself as he resumed his seat. They'd worked hard on this bust of one of the biggest Ecstasy suppliers in the neighborhood—before Prom Night, a real plus—and the judge had just sentenced him to ten years. "We done good," he said to his partner, now seated at the adjacent desk. "And am I glad to have you back, Sal."

"Shahna asked if she could come to work in my place

while I took care of the baby," he said with a chuckle. "I respectfully declined."

Jackson's answering smile turned into a yawn. He needed to get home. He was tired—he and Sal had been up early on a stake-out before attending court, and he wanted a shower, a meal and his bed. He also wanted to check in on Vanessa, see how she was doing.

Which reminded him. He found the file on Ray Ortiz, hoping desperately to find something to pin on him. Jackson wouldn't rest until the man was behind bars for a good long time.

Ray was thirty-six, began life in San Diego, moved up to Montebello, a mostly Hispanic community near downtown L.A., as a child. He'd served two years for dealing. After being released, about ten years before, he'd made his way to the Boyle Heights area of L.A. Since then, he'd been brought in three times for questioning, arrested once. But nothing ever stuck. Lack of evidence, or witnesses intimidated into withdrawing their testimonies.

Jackson set the file down, sat back in his chair. Did he know anyone in the Hollenbeck precinct, where Ray plied his trade? He'd have to check that out, maybe ask Mac, see if he knew anyone. Lots of attempts had been made, but no one had yet managed to catch Ray cold yet with enough evidence to lock him up for a long, long time.

But Jackson would. For Vanessa's sake, he had to.

She was making a big pot of vegetable soup and trying to decide between dried cilantro and dried rosemary for that extra zing when she became aware of shouting from the boys' room. Usually she let Shane and Thomas work things out between themselves, so she waited with one ear cocked, while she chose cilantro.

The noise escalated. When she heard something that sounded like furniture being moved, she turned the heat down under the soup and walked toward the rear of the apartment. At the door, which was closed, she heard Thomas crying, "Gimme that, Shane."

His brother's response was almost too low for her to hear but it matched Thomas's intensity. "Fool. You are such a fool."

"Gimme, Shane, I mean it. It's mine."

There was more noise, a chair being scraped, Shane saying, "You take stupid pills?"

She knocked sharply on the door. "What's going on in there?"

Abruptly, all movement ceased and silence fell. A long silence. She knocked again. "Shane? Thomas?"

When they didn't reply, she opened the door, just in time to see Thomas's hand slip out from under his mattress. He sat on his bed, angry tears still streaking his cheeks, even as he made an attempt to look blasé.

She crossed her arms over her chest. "What is it?"

Thomas's expression turned furtive; then he sneaked a glance at his brother before casting down his eyes. "Nothing."

She turned her attention to Shane, who was shaking his head. "Show her, doofus," he told his brother.

"Stop calling me that!"

"Show her, I said."

Vanessa raised an eyebrow, waiting. "Show me

what?" Something to do with sex, she figured. A porn magazine maybe.

Scowling, Thomas got off his bed, reached under his mattress, and pulled out a small gun.

Taking an involuntary step back, she splayed a hand over her heart. "Oh, my God. Is it loaded?"

"No, Mom," Thomas said with disgust. "I know better than that. I have the bullets in a separate box."

She marched over to him and snatched the thing out of his hand. "What in the world do you think you're doing?" she asked him, as furious as she'd ever been with him.

His chin jutted out. "I'm taking care of you."

"You're what? Where did you get this thing?"

He lifted one shoulder. "Some guys at school."

"Who?" When Thomas pressed his lips together, she glared at Shane. "Did you know about this?"

"Of course not," he said with disdain. "After Khalid shot himself with his dad's gun last year? No way I'm touching the fool things."

She turned back to Thomas, fury waging with fear. She raised her hand, palm up. "Give me the bullets."

Still scowling, he reached into his backpack and pulled out a box which he handed to her. The look in his eye was mutinous. No more sweet twelve-year-old; he was about to disappear into teenagehood, and she hoped she'd survive having two males in that state at the same time.

"You're grounded," she said sharply. "I'll decide for how long when I calm down."

"But, Mom—" tears began to flow again "—I wanted us to have some protection if Ray comes back."

Oh, God. She took a minute to get her pounding

heart to slow down before saying, "I'm touched, Thomas, really I am, and I know you meant well. But you know how I feel about guns. I'm sorry, but what you did is not acceptable."

Back in the kitchen, she set the gun and box of bullets on the table, then threw a dish towel over both. She would have liked to check to make sure the thing wasn't loaded, but she had no idea how to do that without risking injury. When it came to weapons, she was clueless.

She sat down on a chair, heart still thumping at a pretty good rate, grateful that Katy wasn't home—she was at a friend's on a play date. Resting an elbow on the tabletop, she put her forehead in her hand and closed her eyes. So many feelings and pictures were roiling about inside her, she just had to calm down. Thomas's face when he told her he was taking care of her. A different look—mutiny. Shane's disgust with his brother— thank you God—and her horror at the sight of the gun.

Her heart could break in two that her little boy had decided she needed protection and had taken matters into his own hands. An act of love that could just as easily have turned into an act of death. But she had a rule about guns and all the kids knew it.

Maybe she really ought to consider moving, getting her kids away from the city streets, the potential for drugs, guns, violence—the danger that was all around them. Was there a place for them? A small town some-place where the twenty-first century and its potential for instant death hadn't yet become commonplace? Or was that, too, a myth? And even if it wasn't, how could she and her kids fit in? Was there anyplace on earth where race didn't matter?

The eternal question.

She shook her head. Enough. She needed to concentrate on what was happening right now. Thomas had brought home a gun and she needed to deal with it.

She knew what she had to do. She found her new cell phone in her purse and placed the call.

Chapter 7

Jackson slammed his car door then hustled over to Vanessa's building, where he punched in the number of her apartment. She'd sounded upset but had refused to tell him over the phone what had happened. Was it Ray? Had he made any more threats?

She was waiting for him at the door to her place, and the minute she saw him, she threw her arms around him. He held her close, feeling the rapid beating of her heart against his chest and wondering what had brought her to this state.

He stroked her hair; as always, it smelled of lemons. "It's okay, I'm here," he murmured, momentarily allowing himself to enjoy the sensation of her body pressed against his, her being glad to see him, her needing him.

After a short while he felt her take in a deep breath then let it out. Then she stepped back and he followed her inside, shutting the door behind him. "Thanks for coming," she said, sitting down at one of the kitchen chairs.

He took another, noting that the place was unusually quiet. "Where are the kids?"

"Katy's at a friend's. The boys are in their room."

Jackson nodded, noting that she was having a tough time looking at him. "What's going on, Vanessa?" When she didn't answer right away, he said, "Look at me, okay? I just broke my butt getting over here and I'm scared for you. Tell me what's up."

She looked up then. Those clear green-blue eyes were troubled, unsure. "Before I tell you, I need you to promise me something."

"If I can, I sure will."

"I need you not to be a cop now. I need you to be a private citizen."

He frowned. "Can't do that, sorry. I *am* a cop and I'm *not* a private citizen."

She stared some more at him, then seemed to make up her mind. "Fine." She rose, walked over to the door, stood to one side, her arms folded under her breasts. "I'd like you to leave."

He sat back in his chair and gazed at her. "Can't do that, either. Tell me what's going on. And by the way, I'm not leaving until you do."

They had a little staring contest then, but he knew he'd win. She was troubled and needed to blurt it out, whereas he'd been told he could be downright mule-headed.

Finally, she shook her head in disgust and, indicating a faded dish towel sitting in the middle of the table said, "Look under there."

He lifted it up to see what looked like a Smith & Wesson .38. He stared at it, then back at her. "Okay," he said, keeping his voice even. "Where'd you get that?"

"It's not important."

"Oh, I think it is."

Her nostrils flared. "I asked you here so you could check and make sure it's not loaded. And then I wanted to know if you could...get rid of it. You know, isn't there someplace where people can, I don't know, donate guns they don't want?"

He picked up the piece by the muzzle, walked over to the back door and pushed it open. Pointing the instrument away from the house, he carefully released the safety and peered inside. When he returned to Vanessa, he said, "It's empty."

She closed her eyes. "Thank God."

"It's warped, though, a piece of junk. You fire it, it could blow up in your face."

She shuddered, bit her lip, but remained silent.

"Which one?"

"What?"

"Which of the boys brought it home?" When her mouth thinned, indicating she would not answer, he shoved the small gun in his jacket pocket. "Come on."

When she saw him walking over to the front door, she said, "Where?"

"Let's take a walk. We have things to discuss."

She considered him for a moment, then nodded.

"Shane, Thomas," she called out. "I'll be back in a few minutes."

The door to the boys' room opened, and Thomas came barreling out. When he saw Jackson, he stopped short, his eyes big as saucers. Then he looked at his mother. "Why is he here?"

"Jackson and I are going to take a walk around the block. Keep studying, okay?"

The boy stuck his lower lip out. "Am I busted?"

"Did I say anything about that?" she said sharply. "And be quiet. Don't say anything else."

He darted another quick look at Jackson before nodding. "Okay," he said, before scooting back to his room.

It was the time of day when the setting sun was still visible but its light was weak. As Jackson and Vanessa walked along her street of rundown apartment buildings, passing a single, scrawny tree with some pink flowers on it, he kept his hands in his windbreaker pockets, his cop's third eye taking note of anything that looked suspicious. But all he saw were people walking dogs and cars passing by. He took a little time to gather his thoughts, shooting the occasional glance at Vanessa. She was wound pretty tight, no doubt about it.

Finally he said, "It's okay. I'm not going to run him in."

"But you're a cop, as you just reminded me."

"I'm also a man who gets where you're coming from. Want me to talk to him? To both of them?"

"I already have, trust me."

"Even so..."

She seemed to think it over, then nodded. "It will have more impact coming from you."

"Fine. Good thing it wasn't Katy."

"She's only six," she protested.

"They're starting younger every year."

She shuddered. "I don't want to know that."

"No, you don't."

Shadows cast by a row of tall trees across the street put them in temporary shade as they continued on, but they were soon back in the light. On a bus bench, a man slept, a newspaper covering his face. Two women joggers passed by, each talking on their cells via headsets. He wondered briefly if they were talking to each other.

"So, what will you do with it?" Vanessa asked him.

"The gun? I'll take care of it. But I'd also like to get you one just like it, legally, but one that works. And teach you how to use it."

She stopped, stared at him. "Use a gun? Never. Apart from anything else, I have kids in the house."

"It can be locked up, the bullets stored in a safe place."

She shook her head. "Why are you even suggesting this, Jackson?"

He clamped his hands around her upper arms. "Because you're in danger," he said with quiet intensity. "From Ray."

"You don't have to tell me that."

"And I'm terrified for you."

Her expression softened slightly, her eyes warmed. "Thank you. Thank you for caring so much."

"I do."

There was a moment there when their gazes locked and in that moment, it really clicked in how very much he did care. Too much. Way too much.

Vanessa was the one who came back to earth first. "No guns, sorry. I would worry about it all the time. It's like knowing there's a snake somewhere in the house. I'd never get any sleep."

Dropping his grip on her arms, he took her hand in his and they began to walk again. "Snakes are by their nature lethal. It takes a person to make a gun lethal."

"You sound like a recruiting poster for the NRA."

"I may not agree with a lot of what they say, but when it comes to defending yourself against a man with no compunctions about nearly killing a pregnant woman with his fists, then yeah, I'm all for guns."

"And that's supposed to make me feel better?"

"I guess it doesn't. Speaking of lowlife drug dealers and woman beaters, heard any more from Ray?"

"No, but his wife paid me a visit."

Now it was his turn to stop short, and when he did, he dropped her hand. "Excuse me?"

"Sharon Ortiz followed me into the grocery store. She was campaigning for Katy, which I'm sure was Ray's idea. She's a pitiful mess and I felt sorry for her. But he's pulling out all the stops, Ray is."

"Dammit, you need to get a restraining order."

Hands on hips, she glared at him. "Are we back to that?"

"Short of taking out a contract on the miserable son of a bitch or you getting a gun, yeah, we are."

Vanessa hated the turn the conversation had taken,

but she had to admit that Jackson was right. She had to do *something*. "But Ray hasn't laid a hand on me."

"Doesn't have to. He threatened you. At the awards ceremony. And at the lawyer's office. I was there both times. And the other day, back in the alley where you park your car. Didn't you say you had a witness, one of your neighbors?"

"I thought there had to be—what's the expression? Bodily harm?"

"You want to wait for that?"

She felt a shudder go through her. "No. But I told you what happened last time."

"He threatened to come after your kids. But you were alone back then. And you weren't seeing a cop. You have me now, Vanessa, and if you have me, you have an entire force behind you." His face was all hard planes and fierce determination.

"Will that be enough?"

"It'll be enough. Call Shannon. Get that restraining order. Meantime I'll get you some protection. People owe me favors. We'll get a dead bolt on your doors, front and back. And you have all my numbers programmed into your cell, right? 911 too?"

"Yes and yes." She splayed a hand across her rapidly beating heart. "I was frightened before, now I'm scared stiff."

"Good." He put his big hands on her shoulders, squeezed. His blue eyes bored into her soul. "You need to be careful, every moment of every day. Don't walk to or from your car alone, morning and night."

An elderly couple, both of them using walkers,

needed to get by, and she and Jackson automatically moved onto a grass strip by the curb.

"I wish I could just take the kids and get away," she said.

"Why don't you?"

"It's the end of the school year. I can't do that." She reached up and covered one of his hands with her much smaller one. "Jackson, please. He wants Katy. I can't believe he would hurt me. He knows it will go against him if he does."

"And violent people don't always act logically or sensibly."

"I'll be careful, I promise. What more can I say?"

He slid his arms around her, drew her close, pressed her head to his chest. She wrapped her arms around his waist and just stood there, feeling all his strength, all of his determination to protect her, and let it wash over her and bring whatever comfort it could.

Would it be enough? He'd said it would, but she wasn't sure. Really, how could she be?

He moved his lips to nuzzle her neck. "You can say you'll arrange some time to be alone with me. In the next couple of days."

She drew back, stared at him wide-eyed. "Wow, talk about a change of subject."

Draping his arms over her shoulders, he locked gazes with her. The intensity was still there, but now it was of a different type. "I want you, Vanessa," he murmured. "I ache with wanting you."

Her body heated up under his hot gaze. "I want you, too," she found herself saying.

Nostrils flaring, he nodded, pleased with her response. "How about this Saturday? Come to my place."

"What about the kids? I can't protect them if I'm with you."

One side of his mouth quirked up. "How about I get a babysitter for you? One you'll feel comfortable leaving them with?"

"A babysitter? Shane would be mortified."

"I'll take care of that, too."

"You're taking care of everything, it seems," she said, adding, "And I kind of like it."

"Glad to oblige."

A little thrill of excitement rippled over her skin at the thought of being alone with Jackson. She moved into him again, wrapping her arms around his waist. "Do that thing with my neck," she said.

When he nuzzled the skin right behind her ear, she let out a deep sigh, then said, "Who?"

"Who what?" he murmured.

"Who will you get?"

He chuckled softly. "Trust me, okay? Your children will be safe."

She'd never been to his place, which turned out to be a small guesthouse in the rear of a much larger home located a couple of blocks from the beach. It consisted of one large room plus kitchen and bath, and as Jackson took her sweater and tossed it on a wooden hat rack by the door, she said, "Wow, are you lucky to be this close to the ocean."

"Sure am. Been here since I got to L.A. My landlords

are a couple of eighty-year-olds who live in the big house. They don't raise my rent much because they're happy to have a cop on the premises."

He grinned at her and she smiled back, although it wasn't quite as full as his. If part of her was giddy with excitement—and it was—another part of her was nervous. First-time jitters, Jackson had said a while back, and, ludicrous as the expression might be when applied to a reformed hooker, it was apt.

Of course, it helped that he looked wonderful. He wore jeans and a beige cotton cable-knit sweater, the fabrics hugging and outlining that big, broad body of his. The big, broad body that, tonight, she would get to know much more intimately.

He was clean shaven and had gotten his hair trimmed. He'd made an effort for her, as had she for him. She'd bathed in bath salts she'd gotten last Christmas and had never opened. She'd also dressed in low-slung jeans and a cropped sweater; underneath she wore her prettiest underwear. She'd shaved her legs, slathered her body with cream and done all the things a woman does before meeting her lover.

Her lover.

The unspoken word made her insides jumpy all over again, so she busied herself walking around and taking in the simple furnishings of Jackson's place. A small kitchen had pale-blue tile and white appliances. A dark leather couch and easy chair sat across from shelves containing a sound system, a TV, and lots of books. In the far corner was a king size bed with a navy-blue spread. The whole place was on the

messy side but not dirty. More well used. A definite
guy place.

"How'd you like the babysitters I got you?" he asked
with a grin.

"Very clever," she said with an answering smile.

At 6:00 p.m. Lupe, Mac and Wanda had shown up at
her place, ready to take the kids out to dinner, then back
to Lupe's for the night. On Sunday they would all be
going to Disneyland. Jackson's "babysitters"—a retired
cop, his strong-as-steel wife and the kids' beloved
aunt—had her complete and total trust.

"Thought you'd like them," Jackson said now.

Out of nowhere, something fuzzy wound its way
around her ankles and she gave a startled, "Oh." She
glanced down to see a black-and-white cat, which she
picked up and held close, cuddling it like a baby. Its purr
was something pretty special. "Why didn't you tell me
you had a cat, Jackson? I love animals."

"How come you don't have any pets?"

"We used to. The prettiest calico cat. She got out and
just never came back. It's too hard to keep one inside—
the kids are always leaving the door open."

"Ol' Rhonda comes and goes as she pleases."

"Rhonda?"

"That's what the rescue place said her name was, and
I kind of liked it so I kept it. Got her at three months old."

A big, tough guy with a small, fluffy cat that he got
at a rescue place. Jackson and his contradictions. She
smiled at the image as she walked over to a window,
scratching a pleased Rhonda under the chin. She heard
the sound of the refrigerator door opening, then Jackson

said, "I'm getting myself a beer. I have cola, tonic water, oj. What's your pleasure?"

"Tonic water sounds nice." Maybe it would settle her decidedly unsettled stomach.

When would it happen? Who would make the first move? Just how brave was she feeling tonight?

"Oh, and for dinner?" Jackson said. "There's a terrific Mexican joint just down the street. Unless you want to eat fancy, then we got some great steak and fish places."

"Mexican's fine." If she could keep anything down.

He brought her a tonic with a twist of lime in it, then tapped it with his beer bottle. "To tonight."

She nodded, managed to get out, "Tonight."

He studied her face for a couple of silent moments. "You nervous?"

"Yes."

"Me, too."

"Really?"

He cocked his head to one side. "What, a guy can't have a few first-time jitters?"

He was trying to put her at ease, the dear man. "It's my first time in a very long time," she said wryly. "I have a feeling that the same couldn't be said about you."

He chuckled. "No comment." He raised a hand and stroked his knuckles over her cheek, his touch so gentle that she wanted to cry. "Hey, darlin', we won't do anything you don't want to do."

"I know."

"It's not like I'm pushing you or forcing you, am I?"

"No, not in the least."

"Which means at least part of you is glad to be here. With me. Alone. No kids. No worries."

"Most of me, actually, is very pleased to be here with you."

He gave her a sly grin. "In that case, I'd like to do something now I've wanted to do since I met you."

"Oh, God, what?"

The look of sheer horror on her face made Jackson remember that Vanessa had zero sense of humor about the situation, so he cautioned himself to keep it light and easy. He took the cat and set it down on the floor, then removed her drink from her hand and set both his and hers on a side table. Finally, he swooped her up into his arms, plopped down in his easy chair and settled her on his lap, pulling her legs up so they were curled on his thighs. When he eased her head down onto his shoulder, he realized her body was stiff as a board.

"I'm done now," he whispered in her ear.

She didn't respond at first. Then a small voice said, "Nothing else?"

"Nope. Just wanted you curled up in my lap. Thought you'd fit, and you do."

He felt the tension easing out of her fast as melting snow during the first Spring thaw. She even let out a contented sigh. "You smell good."

"Old Spice. Just like my daddy wore."

He stroked her soft hair, which she'd worn loose this evening. She'd obviously dressed to please him, the vee of her top revealing some cleavage, her well-worn jeans hugging her luscious curves, showing a gently rounded stomach, a little enticing belly button. There had been no attempt to hide her womanliness, which made him feel good. It meant she trusted him, somewhat, at least.

He pulled her closer, lost himself in the lemony smell of her hair. "So what did you think I wanted to do?"

"I wasn't sure. I hoped you wouldn't surprise me in a bad way."

"Like all of a sudden reveal my secret life as a cross dresser or foot fetishist?" When she raised and lowered her shoulders, he said, "But you know me, Vanessa, and you know I'm a pretty straight-ahead guy."

"Sometimes men can fool you. Sex makes them… different."

Even as he felt compassion for what she must have gone through in the past, he couldn't ignore the small dart of hurt her comment caused. She'd lumped him in with "men." Again. How long would it take him, he wondered, to completely win her trust?

She must have sensed his reaction, because she added, "But from everything I do know, you're a good man, Jackson."

"As good as the next guy, I'm guessing. Got a bad temper sometimes, get impatient, say the wrong thing."

Raising her head from his chest she gazed at him, her expression serious. "But you like yourself, don't you." It wasn't a question.

He thought about it for a moment. "Pretty much, yeah."

"That's from having such good mothering. That's what I'm trying to do with the kids. Make them feel well loved."

"And you're doing a fine job. It can't be easy."

She returned her head to its snuggling position and he wrapped his arms around her. "In the beginning when Katy was little and Thomas was six and Shane eight and I was struggling with staying clean and getting a job and finding a place to live, oh, God, it was a nightmare. I cried myself to sleep pretty much every night. I had no idea what a good mother was supposed to do or how to act. People say it's natural, but I'm not sure. I had no role models, except for Lupe when I was older."

"Whatever you've done, it's worked. They're great, all three."

"I worry about Shane—he's so closed off."

"Goes with the territory. At his age I was a holy terror."

"You?"

"Oh, yeah." He ran his palm up and down her back, feeling the slimness of her. "Acted out my need to snip that umbilical cord all over the place. Cut school, flunked a couple of classes, did a little joyriding. Got into some fights, stole some from a local farmer. Oh, yeah."

"I don't want to hear this. I don't want to know what's ahead."

"Every kid's different. I got through it, so will Shane."

He needs a daddy, though.

Jackson nearly said it out loud, but stopped himself just in time.

Before she'd come over this evening, he'd paced his floor some, thought about what was going on. He'd made a firm commitment to himself to hold back on anything that sounded like he was future-planning with Vanessa. Not the right time. If ever. If he'd said the other day that he ached for her; tonight, it was more like a hunger, a *craving* that needed release. But he needed to hold himself in check—with her skittishness about what she called "normal" sex, he had to let her set the pace.

Maybe, he'd wondered, all those feelings he got when he was with her were because of plain old frustration, and maybe it was more than that. But there would be no commitment talk tonight, no where-are-we-headed discussions.

First things first. He had this incredible, hot woman on his lap. He slid his mouth up and down her long, velvet-soft neck. "Hungry yet?"

"Not really. I had an apple a little earlier."

"Me, neither. I went in to work for a few hours today and it was one of the secretaries' birthday, so I had me some cake. Two pieces actually. I'm still kind of full."

Talking had relaxed her, but now that they were here, at the point of the evening, he sensed a return of her tension. He decided to kiss it away. Cupping the back of her head he turned her face toward his and did just that. He kept it gentle, unthreatening, using his tongue to trace every part of that luscious mouth of hers. Slow, he cautioned himself. Stay in a low gear, no matter what. This was her first time in a very long time. And the last time had been after a series of men had paid her for it while living with an abusive little prick who, from what Jackson could tell—surprise, surprise—had been as self-involved and brutal in bed as he was in every other part of his life.

So this time had to be good. He *had* to make it good for her, *had* to.

Vanessa gave herself over to taking pleasure in Jackson's kisses, which were skilled and slow and sensual. They'd been down this road before, this and more, that night in his car. But a small part of her tension came from the fact that, tonight, she knew how this would end: he would enter her. From her first violent indoctrination into sex at fourteen, she'd felt intercourse as an unwelcome invasion of a private place, her core, the essence of who she was. Nothing in the ensuing years had changed her mind about that, and she'd turned to drugs to blur reality.

As part of her rehab she'd attended a rape survivors' group, had gotten past whatever guilt she'd been harboring that something about her had caused it. And as the years had gone on, she'd come to understand that most other women reveled in the act of penetration, found their power in giving their most intimate selves to their lovers.

It had never been like that for her. Never.

As the kiss went on, she smoothed her hand over the muscles of Jackson's arms. Strong and hard. So sturdy. And yet, for such a big man he really could be so tender. And that thought gave her the strength to break off the kiss, ease herself off his lap and stand before him. From this position, she was taller than he was, so her next words were surprisingly easy to say.

"How would you feel about us getting naked?"

His strikingly blue eyes widened with surprise before his expression became all simmering heat. "Well, now," he drawled, sitting back in his chair and running his gaze up and down her body, "that sounds just fine with me. And, as I am a true Southern gentleman, I insist the lady go first."

She smiled, ran her tongue over her mouth, knowing

it was provocative, and feeling pleased with herself when she saw the swelling behind his jeans zipper. She held his gaze as she said, "All right."

She reached for the hem of her sweater but before she got very far, Jackson said huskily, "May I undress you?"

She paused, lowered her arms, surprised. Back in her street days, she always did most of the work. "I would love that," she said, meaning it.

Now he stood, took her sweater from the bottom and pulled it up over her head, threw it on the couch. Then he stepped back, gazed at her in her bra, which was pink and lacy.

He shook his head. "Your body is a thing of wonder, darlin'."

"I've had three kids," she said ruefully. "It shows."

"And it makes you even more beautiful, to me."

The smoldering heat in his eyes grew stronger as he unsnapped her jeans, pulled down the zipper and eased the denim fabric down over her hips. When she stepped out of them he tossed them on the couch, too.

Now he took his time feasting his eyes on her entire body, which, besides causing a twinge of embarrassment, was much more of a turn-on than she'd expected it to be. He was taking his time, something else she wasn't used to.

"The first time I saw you," he said, "I thought your skin was like gold."

"Oh." What a lovely thing to say.

He stepped closer again, and his broad hands began at her neck, smoothed over her shoulders and slowly outlined her shape. She closed her eyes, giving herself permission to thoroughly enjoy the sensation of firm hands tracing her arms, ribs, waist, hips, thighs, feet.

She'd polished her toenails and worn a toe ring. "Hmm," she heard him say as he placed her hands on his shoulders for balance before lifting one foot and kissing each toe. "Maybe I will be a foot fetishist after all."

That got a chuckle from her. He set her foot down, reached up and slid her panties down. Now he was seeing the faint silvery stretch marks on her stomach, and when he saw her breasts he would see the same marks there. But somehow Vanessa knew he wasn't one of those men who demanded a perfect body. If he was, she wouldn't be with him today.

So far, so good, she thought, as her heartbeat sped up and blood rushed to the surface of her skin. More than good. Suddenly she wanted him to kiss her. Right there. On the inside of her thighs, on the patch of hair that formed a vee between her legs. To feel the rough surface of his tongue there, around there, in there.

"Jackson," she said, her voice coming out all husky.

"Yes?" He reached behind her and unfastened her bra, skimmed it down over her arms.

She opened her eyes to see him slowly shaking his head in wonder before murmuring, "Your breasts—all of you—you are so beautiful."

She'd been called sexy, hot, but not beautiful. Never beautiful. "My knees are shaking," she admitted as he continued staring at her.

"Jitters?"

"Some. Mostly, it's because I want your hands on me."

He let out a silent whistle. "Works for me." He lifted

her up effortlessly, as though she weighed five pounds, brought her over to the large bed, laid her down on top of it. He stood over her. Smiled. "Is it time for me to get naked now?"

She rose up on her elbows. "Do you want me to do it?"

"Not this time."

"Do I get to look at you the way you did me?"

"Nothing would please me more, darlin'."

He didn't exactly do a striptease, just took his time pulling the knit shirt over his head, getting out of his jeans. And, oh, yes, his body was fine, better even than she'd imagined it. All beautifully defined muscles, long, strong legs, flat stomach, not a hint of love handles. Solid, big. All over.

He kept on his jockeys, which weren't at all successful in masking a pretty sizable bulge between his legs.

"Why not take it all off?" she asked him with a small smile.

"You think you're ready for that?"

"You bragging, Jackson?" She raised a sardonic eyebrow.

His laugh was a big, hearty one. "You sassin' me, woman?"

She gave a little chuckle of her own. "I'm naked, you have to be, too."

"Well, hell, ma'am, we aim to please."

He removed his jockeys, tossed them, met her gaze.

Vanessa's immediate reaction was a small frisson of fear, but not fear of being able to take him in. He was a big man all over, so the size of his equipment wasn't really a surprise. Nor was the fact that he was fully engorged. But this moment was what she'd been thinking about, the fact that she would be expected to welcome him deep inside her.

"Oh, my."

"Good 'oh, my' or bad 'oh, my'?"

"Just 'oh, my.'"

Slowly he walked toward her. "Remember what I said. We won't do anything you don't want to do."

She moved her gaze to his face, which wore a serious expression. "And you can stop now? If I said stop, you would?"

"Yes."

"Wouldn't it be…painful?"

"Sure. And then it wouldn't be." He sat down on the edge of the bed, took her hand in his. "I'm a grown-up, Vanessa."

Yes, he was. This was Jackson, she reminded herself, not someone from her past, and with that the fear faded. The heat that had been pooling in the pit of her stomach was now spreading all through her like wildfire, causing her to put her other hand over her heart. "Well, I don't want you to stop. Not at all. In fact I want you in me." She was surprised to hear the words come out of her mouth. But they were true.

"You ready for that? So quickly?"

Her nipples felt tight, there was moist heat between her legs, she throbbed to feel him inside her. And all that from just looking at Jackson's muscular, well-endowed nude form. "I'm sort of amazed but, yeah. Touch me and see." She lay back, slowly spread her legs, inviting him to do just that.

She was not just amazed, she was blown away by her words and her behavior. But something had eased up inside. Even as her body tingled, tightened and burned all over, she felt relaxed where it was most important—in her head.

Smiling, Jackson lay down on his side next to her, elbow bent, his head resting on his upturned palm. He used the other hand to stroke her all over, the way he had done previously with his gaze. She closed her eyes and gave herself over to the sensations, which were amazing. Wherever his hand touched, the skin beneath it vibrated. When he licked her nipple she gasped, nearly jumping off the bed.

"You, my beautiful Vanessa, are very, very sensitive."

"I guess I am," she murmured.

Finally his hand found its way between her legs. "We are going to have such a good time, darlin.' I am so lucky you are in my life."

It was just about the nicest thing anyone could have said to her.

"Mmm," he went on, his hand stroking her as he used his tongue on the other nipple. "So wet, so ready for me."

He removed his hand and his tongue and she opened her eyes to see what had happened. He reached into the drawer of the bedside table, pulled out a condom, applied it, then lay down on his back, pulling her toward him, easing her on top of him.

He knew, she thought with wonder. He knew it was less threatening to a rape victim if she had some control. And being on top gave her more control. She felt on the verge of tears. How had she gotten so lucky? she thought, not for the first time, as he slowly and carefully set her down on his erection. There was a moment of being stretched to receive him, and then she was able to sit down all the way.

She was full, oh, so full. She opened her eyes, stared at him. He was watching her carefully through eyes glazed with passion.

"You okay?" he asked.

"Yes."

"Sure?"

"Oh, yes," she gasped, because she was, truly, okay. Sensations moved through her like rockets. "I'm not a virgin."

"In some ways you are."

That did it. The tears came, on top of all these sensations. She wanted to sob, to laugh, to scream.

"It's all right, darlin'," Jackson said, clamping his hands on her hips and moving her up and down, setting up a rhythm. Tears streaking her face, she got her knees under her and took over, creating a rhythm of her own. Lord, she was hot! So hot deep inside in that core she'd been thinking about. Yes, he was invading her, and it was fine. More than fine. He was welcome there because he wouldn't abuse her trust.

"Oh, Vanessa," he groaned. "You feel so damned good."

He reached a hand between their legs and used his thumb to stroke her. She was on fire, the flames coming from deep, deep inside. She climbed, her breathing became labored. She climbed some more. Muscles tightened and tightened some more until she couldn't breathe. With a roar, something burst inside her and she was engulfed by the flames. As though from a distance, she heard herself crying out over and over again. Within moments, Jackson's body spasmed, and she managed to tighten her muscles around him, to give him as much pleasure as she could while he came inside her.

And then he was with her, on a long groan that ended with him calling out her name.

Chapter 8

As she was getting ready to go out to dinner with Jackson, Vanessa gazed in the bathroom mirror, saw lips swollen from his kisses, eyes that said she was a satisfied woman, and she shook her head in wonder. What a total surprise this had turned out to be. She really *hadn't* known, had she? It wasn't about her first sexual encounter since before Katy, it was about the first time she'd been with a man who truly thought of her as an equal in bed. A man who put her pleasure before his. It had been a shattering experience for her.

And it terrified her.

She was now in a weak position where Jackson was concerned. She had feelings for him. She *needed* him, had come to depend on him. Way too much, probably. It was scary to need, to want to trust. She had a lifelong pattern of not trusting men, and that couldn't be changed, not in—how long had they known each other?—just over a month? Should she, could she actually trust Jackson? Yes, he cared about her. She got it. It was in every action, every word, every look in his eye.

But for how long? There were so many ways it could go wrong.

She stared again in the mirror, and told herself to stop frowning, stop thinking about the way it could go wrong and enjoy tonight. She'd been given a gift, a few moments in time of being cherished, and she'd be a fool to let that slip away without tasting every bit of it.

They went out to dinner and they both ordered taco plates, Jackson winding up eating all of his and half of hers. They laughed; they held hands; he threw his arm around her on the way home. This was what women expected, wasn't it, those *normal* women. A touch, to be treated with care, a hand in the small of the back. She wondered if normal women appreciated just how special their normal lives were.

They went back to his bed, back to the magic they'd both found there, with each other. And soon, in Jackson's arms, and under the spell of his touch, she put away all her fears about their future. It was okay to allow herself one night, one small time out of reality.

The real world would still be there, waiting, no matter what.

Jackson was awakened the next morning by the jangling phone. Groaning, he reached for the offending instrument. "Yes?"

"Is that any way to greet the day?"

It was Mama. He yawned, then said, "What time is it?"

"Time to rise and shine," she said in her chipper morning voice, a thing of wonder.

He squinted at the clock: 7 a.m. Mama had always been an early riser. "Easy for you to say," he complained.

"All right, grumpy-pants. I just want you to know that I'll be in tonight, so I need you to pick me up at the airport."

"Tonight?"

"Got a pencil?"

He scribbled down her flight time and number, then said his goodbyes and laid his head back down on his pillow.

"Who was that?"

He smiled at the lump under the covers. "Good morning," he said to Vanessa. "That was Mama. She's coming in tonight."

Like a shot, she was out from under the covers and sitting up, staring at him in horror. Her hair was all in a tangle, her mascara smeared, her face a bit on the puffy side—and she was the most gorgeous thing he'd ever seen. Vanessa, in his bed, at last.

"Tonight?"

"Yep." He moved his pillow against the headboard, then sat up and pulled her close, running his palms all over her smooth skin, up and over the luscious curve of her waist and hips, thinking he was about the luckiest man on the planet.

"You'll want to spend some time with her," she said into his chest.

"I will, but I want her to meet you and the kids. Tomorrow's Memorial Day, so I have the day off. Any plans?"

She pulled away from him, sat up, faced him again. His gaze raked her all over. God, she had gorgeous breasts. Not high and perky, but lush and heavy from having had children. The nipples were large, a dark rose color. The small pale stretch marks on the outside of both were a turn-on, although he wasn't sure why. They just were.

When he reached over to cup one of her breasts, she slapped his hand away. "Just how much have you told her about me, Jackson? And don't avoid this discussion."

He was disappointed that she wanted to get all serious this early in the morning, but yeah, maybe it was good to get it out of the way. He threw back the covers, rose, stretched and headed for the kitchen to get the coffee makings started.

"Tell me, Jackson," he heard her say behind him.

"She knows your age, that you have a good job, that you're going to school at night, that you're a single mother with three kids, and that we've only seen each other a few times."

"What else? Does she know I'm not white like her son?"

Right to the point, his lady. He filled the carafe with water, dumped it in the coffee maker well. "Not yet."

"When were you planning on telling her?"

He turned around, coffee scooper in hand. She had joined him in the kitchen and was wearing his old blue terry cloth robe, which was way too big on her. She looked angry, scared and very, very young.

He'd thought long and hard about the question she'd posed and was still of two minds about it. He went back to making the coffee; he was always much better after three or four cups.

"Ordinarily if I was introducing someone to Mama," he said thoughtfully, "I wouldn't mention a person's race at all, the way I wouldn't mention their height and weight or if they like country music. But then I pictured the two of you meeting, with Mama not knowing, and I realized it would place both of you in an awkward position. You waiting to see how she reacted, she having a reaction—which she will—and not wanting to appear impolite. And that doesn't seem fair to either of you." He finished setting up the coffee, punched On and turned around to face her, leaning against the counter.

He had no clothing on and he hoped the sight of his nude body pleased her—something he'd much rather explore than all this stuff.

"And?" she said.

"So I'll tell her tonight, when I pick her up."

"Oh. Well, good."

The entire thing was going to be one hell of a balancing act, that much he knew—two very strong women with two very different sets of life experiences. And him as the battleground. Maybe he should introduce them and excuse himself, go off for a cigar for a couple of weeks, let them duke it out.

Or maybe it would be fine and all this fussing was unnecessary.

And maybe pigs flew.

He pulled her to him, nuzzled her neck, something

he loved to do. She had the softest damned skin. "How about we go back to bed and listen to the coffee dripping," he murmured.

She eased away from him. "What about my history?"

"What about it?"

"Are you going to tell your mother about that?" Again, all defiance and insecurity. Not for the first time, he wished he could fix it for her, present a perfect world to her. But neither of them lived in anything like a perfect world.

"Your background is your business," he said evenly. "Not hers."

"So she doesn't know about my past."

He crossed his arms over his chest. "Do you know about someone's past when you meet them for the first time?"

"That's a cop-out."

"I don't think so. Do you tell everyone you meet that you used to do drugs?"

"No."

"Do you tell every new acquaintance that you had to sell your body in order to get those drugs?"

"Of course not."

"Of course not," he agreed. "Because it's not their business. Maybe, as time goes on and you've established a relationship, yeah, maybe you trade secrets then. You women are always doing that kind of thing. And, yes, I'm not saying there won't be a time and place for that discussion with Mama, but you're the one who has to call it. It's your business, Vanessa, and your timing."

She looked at him, seemed to be thinking it over. Then she pulled the robe tighter around her, left the kitchen.

He followed. "What?"

She walked over to the bed, sat on the edge, looked down at her feet, sighed, said nothing.

"What, darlin'?"

He stood over her, and she looked up at him, her gaze totally, achingly defenseless. "How do you feel about it? About the fact that I used to sell my body?"

Oh, Lord, but she was so fragile, he thought, his heart near to breaking for the burden she carried. He sat next to her on the bed, took her hand in his. "I'll be forty years old in a little over a year, Vanessa, and I've seen a lot of the world, been with a lot of women. You want to know about all of them?"

"Not at all."

"That's how it is for me with all the men you've known."

"It's different and you know it."

"Why, because they paid you?"

She nodded.

"I guess there are some who would say that's a line they can't cross, but I can't see it. You have a past, I have a past. We are who we are today because of that past, and that's all I know."

She sighed, leaned her head against his shoulder. "Oh, Jackson, I wish I could accept myself as well as you seem to accept me."

"If it's any help at all, I think you're just about perfect, past and all. And I have pretty high standards." He squeezed her hand, got up to get them coffee. "I take it black. You need cream, we'll need to go out to get it."

"Black's fine," she said. "Meeting your mother, it's going to be awful."

"I surely hope not. Mama's an okay gal, really she is. Got a few blind spots, but then, all of us do."

Vanessa had tried to calm herself, had given herself a pep talk before meeting Lillian Rutherford, but it wasn't easy. Sometimes she was fine with who she was and sometimes she wasn't. She had a long way to go on achieving that easy self-acceptance that Jackson seemed to be so good at. Her mood wasn't helped by the fact that she always had a couple of bad days preperiod every month when she was jumpy and irritable, and, wouldn't you know it, the day she and the kids were to meet Jackson's "mama" was day one of same.

It also didn't help that when she and her children walked into the pancake place on the Venice boardwalk, Katy was cranky and overtired from too much Disneyland and Shane was giving new meaning to the concept of sullen teenager. Only Thomas seemed his usual upbeat self, thank you, God.

From the moment they met, Lillian reminded Vanessa of social workers from her early childhood who had always made her feel ashamed of who she was. Even the women from A Single Voice had intimidated her at first. It wasn't so much the racial differences, because both the social workers and the A Single Voice women had been all over the place, racially, but it was the fact that these were professionals sent to *judge* her, to see if she was good enough for whatever they had in mind. Good enough to be placed in a foster home, good enough to qualify for free lunches, good enough to bring up her own children, good enough to be allowed to exist.

Lillian Rutherford reminded her of those times and those women. She was beautiful. Tall and slender, regal, really, with silver hair, parted in the middle and worn off her face and gathered at the nape of her neck. The hair style set off pearly, barely lined skin, high cheekbones, a long nose and prim mouth. She was all elegance and grace, and Vanessa immediately felt like a commoner in the presence of a queen and then hated herself for reacting as a child instead of the competent, mature human being she knew she was...most of the time.

Lillian's face remained a polite mask as introductions were made. She asked cordial questions about Vanessa's work and what the children were studying in school. The only time she seemed to relax was when her son teased her, and then Vanessa saw a glimpse of a woman with a sense of humor who was actually capable of enjoying herself.

For her part, Vanessa remained quiet. She didn't want to be here. Why had Jackson pushed it so hard, made this happen so quickly? They'd known each other barely a month, had had a few dates, had slept together for the first time only two nights ago.

The thought of which temporarily took her mind off this awful breakfast and made her remember the magic of being in Jackson's arms, the way her body had soaked up his touch like a newly unwrapped sponge in water. She'd liked being in Jackson's bed so very much better than being here today.

"Mommy, Mommy." Katy was shaking her arm, trying to get her attention.

"What?"

"Can we, please?"

"Can we what?"

"Walk along the Venice canals? Please?"

Apparently, she'd been in her head for part of the table discussion. Quickly Vanessa glanced at Jackson and his mother to see if they'd noticed, but Jackson was paying the bill and Lillian was applying fresh lipstick. So she was all right.

"It's fine with me."

"Good plan, Katy," Jackson said. "Up for a walk, Mama?"

"Well, I certainly hope I am. I'm not elderly yet, you know."

"Are you kidding me?" he said with a huge grin. "You got enough energy to make *me* feel old."

The kids ran ahead of the three adults, while Jackson explained to his mother how Venice, California, got its name. "Back in 1904, this man, Abbott Kinney his name was, got ownership of some marshland through a coin toss. He loved Italy, so he recreated the canals here."

The waterways ran the length of three blocks north to south and three blocks east to west, with houses lining both sides. What had begun as modest shacks with docks for tying up rowboats, intended for the working class, was now an enclave of two- and three-million-dollar mansions, some of which housed movie stars and CEOs. But somehow it still maintained its charm, Vanessa had always thought, which was why she and the kids enjoyed walking here. There were always ducks paddling by and sense of peace and quiet, an oasis from the real world.

As the entire party trooped along the pathway next to the first of the canals, Lillian expressed a similar thought, with not quite the same approval. "Such an odd place, right in the middle of everything."

Jackson grinned. "It's one of the things I love about L.A. Offbeat little neighborhoods right in the middle of the city, houses built on what used to be a racetrack or a wetlands or the back lot of a movie studio."

Lillian sniffed. "It's disorderly." She turned to Vanessa and said, one eyebrow arched, "My son has always had a preference for the unusual. He seems to prefer the road less traveled."

Jackson laughed then hugged her. "And Mama isn't sure that's a good thing. 'Disorderly,'" he repeated with a chuckle. "Oh, Mama. Only you could come up with that one." He winked at Vanessa. "If Mama had her way, we would tidy up the whole thing—no more dead ends, the street names would make sense, probably be in alphabetical order, and all the houses would be white with green trim and shingle roofs."

The older woman hit him lightly on the arm. "Now, Jackson, I'm not that bad and you know it. There is always a place for free expression. But, well, there's so much of it out here."

"Exactly," he said, hugging her again.

His accent got thicker the longer he was with his mother, Vanessa couldn't help noticing. And the two of them were close, very close. It made her feel separate, although she doubted Jackson, at least, was trying to send that message. She wasn't really sure about Lillian. She wondered if the "road less traveled" comment had been aimed at her, and then wondered if she was being overly sensitive.

They walked in silence for a while, with the occasional comment about some outlandish bit of architecture or a nice garden. After a while Lillian looked up at the sky. "Coming up a cloud," she observed, which Vanessa assumed translated as "It looks like rain."

"Maybe we all should head back," Jackson said. "Kids," he called out. "How about we turn around."

Katy, who had been racing back and forth quacking at the ducks, came running up with a happy grin. "I love it here," she said, throwing her arms out.

Lillian smiled at her childish enthusiasm, which eased some of the tension inside Vanessa. If Jackson's "mama" could like her kids, maybe Vanessa could reconsider liking her.

The next to join them was Thomas. "Didn't see any needles today."

"Excuse me?" Lillian said.

"Sometimes junkies shoot up here at night, toss the needles into the canal," he said matter-of-factly. "It's bad for the ducks."

As Vanessa winced, Lillian put her hand over her heart. "Oh, I see."

Katy took the older woman's hand and looked up at her. "If you're Jackson's mommy, what do I call you?"

"Mrs. Rutherford," Vanessa said before Lillian could answer. "You know the rule, Katy."

Her daughter cocked her head to one side and continued to gaze up at Lillian. "Maybe I could call you Grandma. If Jackson wants to be my daddy."

"Katy!" Vanessa said sharply.

"I need a daddy," Katy went on, "because my seed-planting daddy is a bad man who used to hit my mommy."

Her face burning, Vanessa grabbed Katy and pulled her away. "Come on. We have to get home. It was nice meeting you, Mrs. Rutherford," she called over her shoulder as she walked briskly away from the canals and toward the car. "I hope you enjoy the rest of your visit."

She was thoroughly, totally mortified. If she could have scripted a worst-case scenario for the first-time meeting of Jackson's mother, she could not have come up with a better one than what had just happened. Shane with his earphones, being rude to everyone. Thomas dropping that little bit about junkies and needles. Katy telling Lillian about her abusive daddy. What had she been thinking about? she chided herself. That she and Jackson might actually have a chance? She was a fool.

Several yards back, Jackson told Mama to keep walking, but he needed to talk to Vanessa, who was rapidly moving away. Lillian slanted him an I-told-you-so look, sniffed and said nothing.

He hauled ass and grabbed Vanessa's arm. "Hey, darlin', don't be upset. It's okay."

She kept walking. "It most certainly is not. That was awful."

"Not really."

"Thomas, take Katy and head back to the car. I'll be right along."

When the children were out of earshot, she glanced back at Lillian, who was keeping a discreet distance back. "Oh Jackson, let's face it. This, you and me, it won't work out. Really, it doesn't have a chance. Look where I come from and where you come from. We all revert back to our roots as time goes on. You know it and so do I. And I don't care which road you travel on, you're still firmly planted in the lily-white South."

"Man, I hate when you do that," he said sharply. "Lump me in with some 'type.' It's damned narrow-minded of you."

"Fine. I'm narrow-minded." She threw up her hands in exasperation. "I'm also out of here. Please apologize to your mother for me." And with that she walked briskly off after her children.

He stood there, staring at her retreating back. Sometimes he just wanted to shake some sense into the woman, tell her to get over herself.

At that moment his mama caught up to him. "I hope she told you that there's no future for the two of you."

"Not a good time, Mama. Don't," he warned.

"Don't tell me not to express my opinion. I'm your mother and I will express my opinion as I please."

Shoving his hands in his pockets, he began to walk, muttering a few curses under his breath before saying, "What the hell. Express away."

"It's obvious that that young woman and her children live in different worlds than the one you were raised in. It's obvious that her children are street smart and that she's had an abusive husband in her past. Look where she comes from, Jackson. Sooner or later we all revert back to our roots, you know."

He had to choke back a grin. Mama might not like knowing that Vanessa had said nearly the same exact thing just a minute ago. Or maybe she'd like it just fine, as they seemed to both agree that the relationship was doomed from the get-go. Well, maybe it was and maybe it wasn't. But he'd be damned if it was because of what had happened here today.

He thought a bit before meeting her stern, concerned gaze. "Mama, hear me and hear me good," he said slowly. "I love you, very much. And you may express your opinion all you want to, whenever you want to. But don't ask me to agree with you, especially when it comes to Vanessa, because I sure as hell do not."

"You're making a huge mistake," she said grimly.

"Then it's my mistake to make. *If* I am making one. And, in my opinion, you are one hundred percent wrong."

It began to drizzle then, and Jackson took his mama's arm and hurried her toward his car.

The women in his life had issues, that was for sure. At the moment, that locked room with them battling it out was sounding a little less like a fantasy and more like one fine idea.

When she talked to Jackson that night on the phone, he used all his many powers of persuasion to get Vanessa to admit, grudgingly, that Mama hadn't said anything particularly awful to her; that Vanessa had come to the meeting not feeling quite herself; and that, all in all, what Thomas and Katy had said was so awful, all they could do was laugh. Which they proceeded to do. The laughter felt wonderful, she had to admit, and helped to reduce the tension she'd been walking around with all day.

When she hung up the phone, she realized that she still might have to give Jackson up in the future, but for now she was awfully glad that he'd refused her invitation to get out of her life. The truth was she really did care about the man. The word *love* had come to mind a few times during their night together, although she'd refrained from saying it aloud. The entire concept scared her to death.

Her cramps were out in full force now. She popped a couple of aspirin, brewed herself some soothing herbal tea and climbed into bed.

The next day Shannon called to say that the restraining order on Ray had gone through, but that he hadn't been served yet as he was out of town. That got her mind finally and completely off what had happened both on Saturday night in Jackson's bed and Monday at the Venice canals.

All at once she was thrust back into the terror of dealing with Ray and protecting Katy.

The call came late on Friday afternoon.

"You serious with this restraining thing, *chica?*" Ray's voice was softly menacing.

She swallowed down her instant and automatic reaction of her insides twisting and tightening at the sound of his voice. "Yes, I am."

"Your boyfriend the cop, he thinks he can keep me away?"

"This is not about him. It's the law, Ray."

His soft chuckle was not amused. "The law. Oh, 'Nessa. You shouldn't have done this. Really, you shouldn't have. Remember, *chica?* Remember how I hurt you, how I smashed your face? That was nothing. You don't know pain like I can give you. Maybe I'll kill you, then Katy will go to me automatically. I'm her father. Yeah, that might be a good thing to do. Just get you out of the way."

Her heart was racing so fast, she could barely breathe. That same terror she'd felt back before Katy's birth had returned. And now that she'd gone to the authorities, made things official, Ray *would* kill her, wouldn't even think twice about it.

Then she remembered: things were different now. She wasn't alone. She had Jackson in her life.

"You ignore that order and you wind up in jail, Ray," she said as firmly as she could. "That will be strike two for you. Remember how in California we have a 'three strikes you're out' law? How you get three felonies and you spend the rest of your life behind bars? Think before you act, Ray."

Over the line she heard an affronted hiss of indrawn breath. "You giving me a lecture now? You, a little *puta* who barely earned her keep?"

His insult enraged her, instantly obliterating the fear. "Your little *puta* has three kids and a real job now, Ray. A real life. Get one of your own and leave me alone." With that, she slammed down the phone.

And right after she did, she covered her face with her hands. Oh, God, what had she done? You never got angry at Ray, never tried to fight back, because he always punished you. He would come after her now. She had no idea how and where, but he would, for sure.

Hands shaking, she punched in Jackson's work number. When he picked up, she said, "Ray just called."

"And?"

"He threatened me. Hinted that he might kill me."

"Son of a bitch! Did you get it on tape?" They'd set up a recording device on her home phone in hopes they could get backup evidence on Ray.

"I'm at work."

"Damn. What exactly did he say?"

"That he might kill me so he could get custody of Katy."

Now Jackson used a word she hadn't heard since her days on the street, followed by, "Do you know where he was calling from?"

"No."

She waited while he apparently deliberated about something. "It's okay," he said finally, "I can still bring him in."

"On my word alone?"

"Yes. Your word is enough to arrest him. If it gets to trial it will be harder to prove, but in the meantime I'll be digging into his life with a microscope. Don't worry."

"Right," she said sarcastically.

"Hey, I told you I got your back. I'll take care of you. Where are you going now?"

"Home."

"Are the kids there?"

"No. They're at Lupe's. She couldn't do the weekly dinner last night, so it got changed to tonight."

"Have someone walk you to your car. A really big guy. Two of them, if possible, okay? And have one of them follow you for a while, to let you know if you're being tailed. Got it?"

"Got it."

"Go to Lupe's. Call me when you get there. Lock both doors there, too. Stay there until you hear from me."

She felt a mixed reaction of relief for having a plan set out for her, followed by instant guilt. "I'm so sorry to bring all this into your life."

"Stop it, Vanessa," he said sharply. "Go. Now."

Jackson put down the phone, seething inside. This scumbag Ray, this pimp and drug dealer, this sorry excuse for a human being—he had to go, and now.

Scanning all the paperwork on his desk without really seeing it, he took in a few deep breaths to clear his brain, and considered his options. He had no idea where Ray was at present, but the obvious thing was to try his Encino home. First, however, he needed to cover his own back.

"Hey, Sal," he called to his partner, who was busy at his desk with his own paperwork.

Sal looked up, his usual upbeat expression gone, his face drawn looking from several weeks of a new baby and night feedings. "Yeah, what?"

"Remember a few weeks ago, when Shahna was having the baby, and you asked me to cover for you at a ceremony?"

"Yeah."

"I need you to do something for me now."

"How much time will it take?"

"Not sure."

His partner heaved a huge sigh. "Let me call home, tell Shahna I'll be delayed."

"She won't be happy."

"Hey, she's a cop's wife. They don't have a choice."

They got right into the middle of late-afternoon traffic, never a pleasant experience, but always worse on Fridays. But Sal was driving, so Jackson tried to relax. His hands were itching, wanting to get themselves around Ray's neck. Good thing for Ray that he was a cop—it was a natural deterrent.

His cell phone rang, and he opened it to hear Vanessa saying, "I'm here, at Lupe's."

He offered a silent prayer of thanks. "Good. Stay there."

"Where are you?"

"On the 405 behind a diesel truck."

"You mean cops need to worry about getting behind a truck?" she asked, her voice shades lighter than earlier. "I thought that was one of the perks of your profession."

"You're absolutely right. Sal—let's go with the siren."

"My pleasure," Sal said, placing the light on top of the car and turning on the siren.

They made it to Encino in ten minutes, turning off the siren and light a few blocks away from Ray's house. At the door of the pseudo-Colonial, Sal punched in the bell, several times. It was opened by a woman, blond and pretty in an anemic kind of way. There was no character and no strength in her face, Jackson observed. A real victim type. Perfect mate for an abuser.

Sal and he showed their badges, then Sal said, "Ma'am, I'm looking for Romeo Ortiz. Is he here?"

Her eyes, already wide with fear, opened wider. "Oh, no, he's not."

"I told you not to answer the door, Sharon" came an annoyed voice from within. "Let the maid do it."

Then Ray appeared in the entryway. He took one look at Sal, then noticed Jackson and tried to push the door shut. But Jackson was already pushing it in, walking into a spacious foyer with marble floors and a winding staircase to the upper stories.

"Hey," Ray said. "You guys can't just barge in like this."

"Up against the wall," Jackson growled, "and spread 'em. And yeah, we can."

While Jackson patted him down, Sal said, "Romeo Ortiz, you're under arrest for ignoring a restraining order and making criminal threats." He then recited him his Miranda rights while Jackson put the cuffs on him.

Ray was spitting with fury. "Sharon, call Constantine. Have him meet me at the jail."

"Not gonna work, Ray," Jackson said.

"I'll get out on bail."

"Not before a judge hears your charge and as it's Friday, everybody's gone for the day."

"I got a right to my lawyer."

"And you'll get him. Just not tonight."

"Ray," the wife said, wringing her hands, "don't say anything, okay? I mean without your lawyer present?"

"Shut up, Sharon," Ray snarled. "Just call my lawyer."

Cursing him and Sal, in both English and Spanish, he was led out to the car. Jackson was not gentle with him as he got Ray settled into the backseat. "You sit with him, Sal. I don't trust myself around this piece of dirt."

While Jackson drove, Ray kept up a constant stream of threats and curses from the rear. "You really think you can get away with this, man?" he said to Jackson. "When I tell the judge you're sleeping with Vanessa, these charges will be thrown out."

Sal said, "Me? Sleeping with her? I'm a married man with a new kid. I'm too tired to even think about it."

"I don't mean you, pig."

"I would be real careful with your language, Ray," Sal said evenly. "We policemen have very tender feelings, and when we're insulted we have all kinds of ways of getting even."

"Watch me shaking. And I don't mean you, I mean the pig who's driving. He's on a vendetta—my lawyer will have me sprung in no time."

"Sal here's the arresting officer, Ray," Jackson said over his shoulder. "Sal's been a member of the LAPD for fifteen years. He's been decorated. He's even a hero. Rescued a couple of kids and a dog from a burning building. This has nothing to do with me. I'm along for the ride."

"Bullsh—"

"Whatever. And I don't care what you think you're going to get away with, Ray, trust me, it ain't gonna happen."

* * *

Vanessa heard from Jackson while she was still at Lupe's with the kids. "He's locked up good and tight," he told her.

She allowed a small surge of relief to flow through her before asking, "For how long?"

"At least the weekend. Maybe for keeps."

"Can you do that?"

"I can sure try."

She closed her eyes. "Oh, God, he'll be so angry."

"I have a call in to the assistant D.A. who happens to be a woman specializing in going after abusers. At the bail hearing on Monday, she'll request no bail. He's had a previous restraining order against you, and he's already served time, so we might be able to make it stick."

She allowed herself to feel a stirring of hope. "You can do that?"

"All I can do is being done, Vanessa. I want you to relax. Whatever else happens, you're safe for the entire weekend."

The sense of relief, of letting go of a tension she'd been carrying for weeks, made tears come to her eyes. "Thank you."

"Just doing my job, ma'am," he said lightly.

"Right."

"When will you be home?"

"About nine-thirty or so. The kids and I were just leaving."

"Want company?"

"Please."

"If I come I want to stay the night. Which means the kids will see me in the morning."

She knew she ought to think hard about this one. But she didn't want to. She wanted to lavish kisses all over Jackson's body. Wanted to let him know how much she cherished his presence in her life.

"Saturday morning is waffles," she said. "Will that do?"

Chapter 9

It was Friday night with no school tomorrow, so Vanessa made a big bowl of popcorn. After Katy was put to bed, the boys and Vanessa sat on the couch, Jackson in their one easy chair, and watched TV. As they did, she was overcome with a sense of *rightness* about the whole thing: Ray was in jail, so there was no threat hanging over her head; two kids and two grown-ups in the living room watched a TV program. A real *Brady Bunch* moment. She had to smile at that one. Exactly like the Bradys. Except, of course, for the fact that she and the kids were multiracial, she'd never been married, was an ex-hooker and druggie, and "Dad" was a burly white cop with a Southern accent. Otherwise, yeah, just your average, everyday American family.

The pleasantness was shattered when, during a commercial, Thomas turned to Jackson and said, "So are you my mom's boyfriend now?"

"Quiet, doofus." This from Shane.

"I'm just asking."

Jackson looked over at her, met her gaze. The ball was in her court, she knew, so she was the one who spoke up. "Jackson and I are dating," she said casually, "yes."

"But, like, is it serious? Is he gonna move in? Are you gonna get married?"

"Hold it right there," she said, darting him a sharp glare. "No one's mentioned marriage yet. We're dating, that's all. Nothing else."

"But we're pretty serious," Jackson said.

She whirled around to face him. "Stop it, Jackson."

"Which is why I'll be staying the night. With your mom."

Thomas's eyes widened, then he put his face in his hands and shook his head. "Gross."

Shane's look of utter disgust was classic. "C'mon, Thomas."

Without a word the two of them walked down the hallway, went into their room and closed the door.

What in the world was wrong with this man? She rose from the couch and stomped over to the easy chair, keeping her voice low as she said, "Why did you say that?"

His jaw was set in a stubborn line. "Because it needed saying."

"Don't you know that children don't like to think of their mothers as sexual beings? I'm Mom, with a capital *M*."

"You have a lover, Vanessa," he said mulishly. "I'll

be here in the morning, and it seemed to me pretty clear that standards need to be set. That we're serious, which is why it's okay for me to sleep with you. Or is that not the lesson you want them to learn?"

"First of all, do you have any idea what lessons my children have already learned? These are not some sheltered, small-town boys—these are street kids, city kids. Half of their friends' parents are divorced, a quarter of them have no father at home, a whole bunch of them have mothers who have all kinds of lovers, from one-night stands to live-ins."

"That doesn't mean kids don't appreciate some standards."

"Well, of course they do, and I'm trying to set standards all over the place. But it's *my* place to do that." She pointed a finger at him. "You can't just barge in here and start doling out daddy lectures. It's not your place. You're not their father."

His head jerked back, as though she'd hit him. Tight-lipped, he said, "You're right. I'm not." He vaulted out of the chair and headed for the kitchen.

She caught up to him at the front door. "We're having a discussion, Jackson. Don't you walk out on me."

Without turning around, he said, "I'm not too nuts about being lectured at, Vanessa."

Hands fisted on her waist, she said, "Well, I'm not too nuts about the way you decide to do things without checking with me first."

He didn't turn around; he was reining in his temper, she could tell. But she could also tell her "you're not their father" remark had wounded him—there was tension in his shoulders, his hands at his sides were clenching and unclenching.

She put a steadying hand on his arm, said quietly, "Jackson, you need to give me time. I don't know what's right here, I'm feeling my way. What you did was you were honest with them. You treated them like adults. I'm not sure that was the best way to do it. It's all happening so fast."

Slowly he turned around, the storm in his blue eyes easing. "Whether they're ready or not, Vanessa, some things need to be out in the open." He sucked in a breath, blew it out, then frowned. "I'm serious about you," he said, grimly.

"You don't seem very happy about the fact."

"Well I am," he snarled. "Damned happy."

She couldn't help herself—she snickered. It was all so ludicrous, this ordinarily tender pronouncement coming out instead like a declaration of war. She covered her mouth with her hand, but the laughter escalated and escaped anyway.

At first Jackson seemed offended, then his expression softened until he was smiling sheepishly. "Okay, okay, I suck at this." He shook his head. "Hell of a way to tell a woman I'm in love with her," he muttered almost to himself.

"What?" Vanessa stopped laughing.

His expression turned serious again. "That just… popped out. But I guess I must mean it."

Her emotions more in an uproar than she showed, she commented dryly, "And again, I don't see any huge amount of joy."

"Well, as you said, it's not exactly a match made in heaven."

"It isn't a match at all, Jackson. Not yet."

He nodded. "Okay, not yet. But we're heading that way. We both know it. We're too good together to ignore it."

She gazed at him for a while, then swallowed down a lump of unexpressed emotion as all of it flashed in her brain in an instant—his mother, their diametrically different backgrounds, all the problems they hadn't even discussed yet. And yet, despite that, she'd never had feelings like this in her life before and they had to be acknowledged. Not to mention the man had just said he was in love with her.

She swallowed again before saying, "Yes, we are good together." Before he could reply she held up a hand. "But that doesn't mean anything. Not in the long run. Good things go wrong."

"And they go right, too."

"Okay, so we have a fifty percent chance at making it. I don't like the odds."

"What are you saying?"

"That we need to slow down. Act like mature adults. Take our time. You *push* me, Jackson. From the beginning, you pushed for a date, you pushed for us to get intimate, you pushed for your mother and me to meet. That was a disaster, it was way too soon. I can't go that fast, I can't adapt that quickly. Change, for me at least, doesn't happen in an instant."

He seemed to consider her words for a moment before nodding. "Yes, I do push. Sometimes I feel like

I'm on the express train and you're chugging along on the local, and it scares me. So I push. I think I'm probably afraid that if I don't, you'll find a reason for us not to end up at the same place, a reason for us not to be together, and that is…unacceptable."

The look in his eyes was so open, so vulnerable, that she felt another lump forming in the back of her throat. Even so, she knew they had to put the brakes on before she got so involved in her feelings for Jackson she would forget her other priorities. "Look," she said. "Why don't we take a little time to think, okay? You muddle my head and that's not good. I imagine I muddle yours, too. You need to give it some thought—consider your mother and her feelings, and if a woman who comes with three kids and a lot of old ghosts is what you really want for your life."

She saw his jaw clench before he said, "Don't you think I've been considering all of that? I don't wear blinders, you know. I've known who you are since day one."

"Maybe so, but you couldn't stand here and tell me you loved me without looking really pissed off. I don't need that."

"Maybe you don't need *me,* then."

"Maybe I don't."

They glared at each other for a moment, then, as though some silent signal had been sent, both of them relaxed their antagonistic postures. Vanessa felt unbearably sad, and tired, too. "I don't want to fight with you, Jackson."

He scratched his head, made a face. "I'm thinking

it won't be a good idea to spend the night after all," he said glumly.

"It's probably better if you go," she agreed. With her hand on the doorknob, she looked up at him. "Give me some time to think, okay?"

Those clear blue eyes of his were shadowed with sadness as he met her gaze, then he pulled her to him, wrapping his arms around her and holding her close. She let herself feel the solid comfort, the strength of him, the mixture of Old Spice and manly body heat, for a few lovely minutes, then she drew back, tried to smile and said, "Go now."

"I'll call you tomorrow."

She reached up and stroked his cheek. "Don't, okay? Like I said, you muddle my brain. We'll talk next week."

She could tell he didn't like it, but he nodded curtly before walking out the door.

She kept herself busy on Saturday. Thomas and Shane went off with some friends, and she took Katy shopping for summer clothing, winding up later at Lupe's. Her aunt was helping Katy with her costume for her school play. The little girl, who was now a whole size larger than just three months ago, was to be an amaryllis, wrapped in a long green stem all the way up to her neck, where a high collar of pink and orange petals would frame her face.

And all that night and into the next day, Vanessa tried to think through the repercussions of a long-term relationship with Jackson, but her head wouldn't cooperate. It wanted to escape, instead, into mindlessness. She cleaned house like a madwoman, watched monotonous

TV instead of studying, did anything that didn't take mental concentration. On Sunday night she had dreams that involved trains and Katy and Jackson and Ray, but when she woke up, she could barely remember them.

Monday morning Jackson called her at work with the news that Ray had been released from jail on bail.

"We tried, Vanessa—the A.D.A. did her best to keep him incarcerated, but Constantine argued and the judge saw it his way. The bail was set pretty high, but Ray's out. And I'm so sorry." His attitude was almost formal, not a hint of affection or intimacy.

"You did what you could." She kept her tone impersonal, too.

On the other end of the line Jackson, waiting with Sal in the corridor outside the courtroom, muttered, "And look how much good that did."

"Hey, don't blame yourself—"

"I'll call you later," he interrupted her. "They're coming out of the courtroom now."

He and Sal stayed a good distance away from the double doors, so when Ray and his lawyer came out, they didn't notice the two detectives. Outside, Constantine shook Ray's hand and walked toward the parking lot. Ray stood on the curb, glancing at his watch, obviously waiting for a ride.

Jackson and Sal walked up and stood on either side of him. "Don't even think about going near her, man," Jackson said in a low voice.

"Piss off," Ray said.

"I mean it. You step one foot near that lady or her family and you're dead meat."

"A cop threatening me?"

"Believe it."

He looked at Sal. "You heard that."

Sal gazed around him, all innocence. "Excuse me? What did I hear?"

Ray's eyes darted around the immediate vicinity, but the two seasoned detectives had chosen their spot well. No witnesses.

Jackson said, "We clear, Ray? You got the message?"

At that moment a large black Mercedes pulled up to the curb—the same one Jackson had seen Ray driving away that first day he'd met him. Sharon Ortiz was at the wheel. Ray yanked open the passenger door, saying, "Took you long enough."

As he got in, his wife was whining about something. When the car was half a block away Ray lowered his window, stuck his hand out, and raised his middle finger.

Jackson and Sal watched them drive away, then Sal turned his attention to his partner. "That's one mean son of a bitch."

"Something bad's gonna happen, Sal," he said, shaking his head. "And I don't know what to do about it."

"Maybe you ought to tell your lady friend to take a little trip, get away somewhere with the kids."

Lady friend? Jackson thought. Not at the moment. Out loud he said, "We already talked about that. She says Ray will find her if he wants to wherever she goes. Besides, the youngest, Katy, has this school thing tomorrow night. It's some kind of big deal. I'll be there." Whether Vanessa wanted him there or not.

Sal grinned. "Oh, man, she got you going to the kid's school play now? You are toast."

Jackson didn't smile back. "That I am, Sal."

Vanessa was surprised that Jackson was actually here at Katy's school with her, the boys and Lupe. The only people who should be forced to watch tiny children attempt to sing and dance were proud family members with cameras—otherwise, it had to be excruciatingly boring. But here he was, as he'd said, to "keep an eye on things," meaning, of course, Ray.

And so he sat, his arms folded across his chest, his eyes constantly checking out the audience, scanning for danger. For over forty minutes they all watched bunny costumes and long beards on short, round children. And then the music came on for Katy's class and their flower dance.

Smiling, Vanessa watched as the line of roses and daffodils and carnations came on stage. As the moments went by, Katy and her amaryllis costume failed to emerge. She waited a few heartbeats longer, then she was up from her seat and dashing down the side aisle. She climbed the stairs to the side of the stage and pushed through the curtain on the far left. The teacher, Mrs. Wu, who had always seemed way too young to be in charge of children, was there, looking frantic.

"Where is she?" Vanessa asked her immediately.

"I'm so sorry Mrs. Garner. I can't find Katy anywhere."

The piano music continued to play while Vanessa tore through the entire backstage area, checking for her daughter. She wasn't in the dressing room or the girls' bathroom. She even knocked on the boys' and went in, but her daughter was nowhere in sight.

When she ran back to the side of the stage, Jackson was talking to the teacher, who seemed intimidated. Lupe and the boys stood to one side, watching with worried looks on their faces. Onstage, the music stopped, there was applause, and one by one the little flower-costumed first-graders came into view.

As each passed her by, Vanessa said, "Have you seen Katy?"

Each shook their head until one little blond girl, dressed as a sunflower, said, "She went with Mrs. Cabot."

Vanessa leaned over and clasped the child's shoulder, cautioning herself to be gentle. "Mrs. Cabot?"

She must not have been gentle enough, or else the tension backstage was affecting everyone, because the child's mouth began to quiver and her large blue eyes filled. "She told Katy that her mommy was sick and she had to come with her."

As Mrs. Wu scooped up the little girl to comfort her, Jackson barked, "Who is this Mrs. Cabot?"

Heart in her throat, Vanessa stood back and let him take over.

"A very nice woman," the teacher said. "She showed up about three weeks ago. She said she lived in the neighborhood and that she and her husband were about to adopt a six-year-old child and were looking at schools. She said she really liked what she saw here and could we use a volunteer? You know how much we always need help, especially with the show, so I said yes."

"Did you check her out?"

"Of course I did," she said indignantly. "She showed me a driver's license, gave us an address and a phone number. I called it, and a maid answered 'Cabot residence' and I asked if that was where Mr. and Mrs. Cabot lived, and she said yes." She burst into tears. "That's what I'm supposed to do, check ID, call and verify residence, and I did."

Another teacher came over and put her arm around Mrs. Wu. "There, there, Connie, it's not your fault."

"We don't care whose fault it is," Jackson said harshly. "Let me see the card she filled out."

"And just who are you?" the new teacher said.

He took out his wallet and showed his badge. "LAPD. Quickly."

"I have to clear it with the principal."

"Where is he?"

"*She* is in the audience."

"Go get her."

But there was no need because the show had stopped due to all the commotion backstage, and a short, gray-haired, grandmotherly woman came bustling in from out front. "Just what is the problem here?"

Jackson explained as quickly as he could. The principal nodded. "Mrs. Wu, will you and Ms. Lemont please tell the audience members that there has been a delay and we'll get back to the show as soon as possible?"

Vanessa, her mind trying not to face reality by remaining blank, took note of the fact that Jackson opened his cell and barked something into it. Then the principal, Jackson and Vanessa scurried to a door that went from the backstage area, down corridors, past small classrooms to the principal's office.

Vanessa held her breath while the older woman thumbed through a box of index cards before coming up with one. Jackson grabbed it from her, then read it. "Sharon Cabot," he said, meeting her gaze.

She sank into a chair, her knees no longer able to hold her. "I thought so," she said dully. "Ray has her."

Jackson opened his cell phone again, punched a button and spoke to someone, reading off the address on the card. "Check it out. I'll hold."

"Are you okay, Mrs. Garner?" the principal asked. "Shall I get you some water?"

"Do that," Jackson snapped, then listened on his phone. "The address is bogus," he told Vanessa. "It's a Ralph's Market." He spoke again into the phone. "Check registration of all vehicles under the name Romeo Ortiz, Sharon Ortiz and Sharon Cabot. *C-A-B-O-T.* Call me back ASAP. We need to issue an Amber Alert."

He snapped the phone shut, knelt on one knee in front of her, took her hands in his. "Tell me all you know about Sharon."

The whirling in her head made it difficult to concentrate. "She's from back east, Ray said. There's family money and she can't have children and that's all I know." Her hand flew to her chest—her heart was pounding so hard she was afraid she was going to pass out.

"Where's that water?" Jackson called out.

The principal came rushing back with a cup and gave it to Vanessa. Her hands were shaking so hard it was difficult to hold on to it.

Jackson's cell phone rang. He listened, nodded. "Two vehicles registered in California—the Mercedes and a motorcycle. Let's go with the Mercedes, and put out an amber alert. She's six, mixed race, curly black hair, brown eyes." He looked at Vanessa. "What was she wearing?"

"A…costume, an amaryllis costume. All green on the bottom with a huge pink flower thing up above, her neck and head sticking up in the center."

"What was she wearing underneath?"

She closed her eyes, picturing her baby before they'd left for school this evening. "Blue shorts, a white T-shirt, white socks and sneakers."

As he repeated all of this into the phone, the sound of sirens were heard outside, coming to a stop nearby. The principal's office was near the school's entrance, and in moments two newcomers—a sandy-haired, medium-size woman carrying an extra twenty pounds, and a slightly taller and much thinner African-American man—came through the door. When they saw Jackson, they hustled over to him. "Hey, Rutherford," the male said, "what's up?"

"Kidnapping. Six-year-old girl. About fifteen to twenty minutes ago, from what we can tell."

"Fill us in," the woman said.

"You got patrolmen at all the doors?"

She shot him a sour look. "We know our job, Detective."

"Okay. Sorry." Then he told them all he knew so far, after which they went off to reinterview the teacher and her children.

Vanessa heard it all as though from a distance. She was gone, somewhere deep inside her head, the part of her brain that housed every terror imaginable, every conceivable nightmare scenario possible when a child has been taken. She could hear her heart pounding rapidly in her ears, echoing loudly in her head, and wondered if she would faint, something she'd never done in her life, even at its worst moments.

"Vanessa?"

She didn't hear him at first.

"Vanessa?" Jackson took her arm and squeezed it gently, but just as with her treatment of the little girl earlier, his tension came through. "We need a picture of Katy."

It was enough to bring her back with a snap. "Yes, of course."

She reached into her purse and withdrew her wallet, then took out Katy's most recent school picture. Jackson snatched it up and gave it to the other cops, who he introduced as Detectives Sandra Pauley and William Lee. They were part of the year-old Emergency Kidnapping Squad attached to his precinct, which was five minutes away, and the fact that they'd both still been at their desks at seven on a Tuesday night was the only good news so far this evening.

As Vanessa nodded to them both, the woman said, "We'll find her, Ms. Garner."

"Please," she managed.

Detective Lee said, "I suggest you go home. This might be a ransom thing."

"No, it's not—I have no money."

"Even so—"

"Look, it's Katy they want," Jackson interrupted. "Not money."

"How do you know that?"

"Sharon Cabot's husband is the child's father, although—"

Now it was Pauley's turn to interrupt. "Hold it right there," she said. "This some kind of a custody dispute? Because in that case…"

Jackson blew out an impatient breath. "This is not some interfamily mess, Sandra. Ms. Garner has sole custody, and a restraining order against Romeo Ortiz, who has threatened to kill her. He's currently out on bail pending trial. Okay?"

He looked at each of them and got a nod. Then he put an arm around Vanessa. "Go home. Take the kids and Lupe. There's nothing you can do."

"What will I do there?"

"What will you do here?"

She had no answer for that, of course.

At that moment, Lupe and the boys were escorted into the principal's office, looks of worry and uncertainty on their faces. Vanessa waved weakly at them, which the boys took as a signal and ran over to her. Lupe, her mouth in a grim line, nodded to her. "Come on, Vanessa. We need to go home. We need to let the police do their job."

For a long time she paced, back and forth, back and forth in the living room, listening for the phone while the boys stayed in their room, Shane lost in his earphones and Thomas playing with a hand-held computer game. In the kitchen Lupe had found some ingredients and was making *albondigas* soup. The smell of onions, hot pepper and garlic soon permeated the entire household.

Vanessa had no idea what to do with herself, where to focus her thoughts so they weren't dwelling on the pictures her mind was creating.

Katy, sobbing and scared.

Katy, crying for a mother who wasn't there.

Lupe came into the living room, set down a cup on the coffee table, then led Vanessa over to the couch. "Sit," she ordered. "I made tea."

In a fog, she picked up the cup. Even though the tea was very hot, it barely registered.

Katy, her crumpled body lying in a ditch.

She set the teacup down, put her face in her hands and sobbed. Lupe sat down next to her and put her arms around her, just as she'd done when Vanessa was a child. It would have been nice if Lupe's embrace could have comforted her now as it had back then, but the only thing that would bring relief was Katy's return, healthy and smiling. Even so, she let herself sag against the roundness of Lupe's breasts and cried her heart out.

After a while there were no more tears. Some of the tension in her body had been released, at least. She sat back up, took another sip of tea. "Thanks, Lupe."

"Jackson is a good man, he'll find her."

Frowning, she turned to her aunt. "What does his being a good man have to do with anything? You think there's some kind of justice in the world? You think life is fair? That just because Jackson's a good man and Ray's a bad man that I'll get my Katy back?"

Lupe took her hand and clutched it tightly. "Oh, *hija*, don't. Don't think about all the bad that can happen. It doesn't help."

"My baby is in the hands of a vicious man and his robot wife. Can you blame me?"

The door to the boys' room opened and Thomas came out, looking young and scared. "Mom?"

She had other children, Vanessa told herself. Children who needed her, and as much as she could, she wanted to be there for them. "Hi, Thomas," she said with a watery smile. "How are you holding up?"

"Jackson will get her back. Just like Aunt Lupe says."

He looked so very young and so very trusting. And if it gave him comfort, if he wanted to believe that, who was she to dispute it?

Beside her on the couch, Lupe was moving her lips silently, which meant she was praying. If only she herself could access the solace of religion, Vanessa thought, or even of God. But in the world she'd known for most of her life, neither had played a huge role.

Jackson insisted on tagging along with Pauley and Lee, and he quickly led them to Ray's Encino house, while they waited for permission to enter by force, if necessary. They were all pretty sure that Ortiz and his wife wouldn't have been stupid enough to bring Katy here, but they had to check. Sure enough, there were no interior lights on when they got there, and repeated poundings on the front door brought no response.

When Lee received the verbal okay over the phone to search the premises, they proceeded. Guns drawn, they broke in and quickly went through the place, following the drill of being prepared for surprises. But there was no one there. Jackson opened the door that led from the kitchen to the garage where he found the black Mercedes and a big Harley-Davidson. The hood of the Mercedes was cold. It hadn't been driven recently.

Back in the kitchen he conferred with Pauley, who put in the call. "The Amber Alert that's gone out on the Garner kid has the wrong vehicle. Do a nationwide on all vehicles registered to the same three names as before—Romeo Ortiz, Sharon Ortiz or Sharon Cabot. And while you're at it, do the same for any real estate owned by the same names. Start with Southern California for now, then neighboring states." She listened, nodded. "Yeah, I know it'll take a while, so start now."

By the time she'd ended the call, Lee had joined them in the kitchen. "Okay," he said, "let's start checking with the neighbors."

At seven the next morning Jackson rang the buzzer to the Garner apartment. Lupe was the one who let him in, a look of hope on her face. "Anything?"

"No," he answered grimly. "Where is she?"

"In her room."

He strode through the living room and knocked on Vanessa's door. "Come in," he heard from the other side.

She was sitting up in bed on top of the bedspread and staring at the partly closed blinds that covered the window. She was barefoot, but was wearing the same clothes she'd had on the night before. In the morning light that leaked through the slats, he could see dark circles under her eyes, and it seemed as though her skin was ashen.

When she saw him, she sat up straighter. "Katy?"

He shook his head. "I thought I'd give you a progress report."

"Fine." Her shoulders slumped again.

Lupe stuck her head in the door. "Coffee, Jackson?"

"Please."

"How about you, *hija?*"

Vanessa shook her head. Her eyes were dull; her hair was in tangles. It was as though, during the night, something had come along to suck all the life out of her. She was in full despair. He'd seen it before, of course, but it made his heart ache.

He sat on the edge of the bed near her feet, then pulled them onto his lap and began massaging her toes. She closed her eyes for a moment, then said, "That feels wonderful."

"Good. Here's where we are," he said, keeping up the pressure on the tight muscles of her feet. "Neither Ray nor Sharon has flown out on any commercial airlines. We contacted the Hollenbeck precinct, which is where Ray deals his drugs, faxed them Katy's picture, which they are distributing all over the place. They're also checking with all their snitches, to see if anyone knows anything. Ray and Sharon own a condo in Palm Springs, but the police down there have checked and no one's there. We're thinking Sharon's car may be registered out of state, so we're looking through every data base east of Chicago, although it's taking us a while to get a response from some states. My captain is thinking of calling in the FBI. As soon as we get a vehicle ID and description, we issue a new Amber Alert."

She opened her eyes, gave him a tired smile. "They're really pulling out all the stops, aren't they? Is it because a cop is a friend of the family?"

"They do this for all kidnapped kids, Vanessa. Even so, yeah, I told them you were my girl and that this was personal."

"The police fraternity."

"That's it. We'll get her."

Lupe came in, handed him a cup of hot coffee before meeting his eyes. "You slept any, Jackson?"

"I'm thinking none of us has. Right?"

She smiled sadly, then walked out of the room.

He turned again to face Vanessa, who said, "I have a question."

"Ask away."

As he sipped his coffee, he could see her steeling herself before saying, "What are the statistics? How many missing children do you actually recover?" She swallowed before adding, "Alive?"

"I don't know. I have no idea." This wasn't his area, for sure. But the lack of sleep had made his brain foggy. He shook his head to clear it. "But hey, we got a couple of things in our favor. First, all of Ray's contacts are here in L.A., so it's unlikely he'll travel with her, try to set up someplace else. That narrows down the search area."

"To a mere what? Seven million people or so?"

"Better than the entire world, Vanessa."

"What else?"

"Ray has no reason to harm her. Just the opposite, in

fact. So some of the other options in these kinds of cases aren't in the mix." He didn't voice any of those options—illegal adoptions to childless couples, child prostitution, kiddie porn. The list went on and on, but Vanessa had been raised in the streets and she knew what they were.

She nodded. "I've thought of that." Out of nowhere her eyes filled with tears. "But Ray can get crazy, and she's my baby, Jackson."

Now his heart cracked in two. He set his coffee cup down on the side table, then slid closer so he could take her into his arms. But she stiff-armed him, shaking her head. "Don't, Jackson. I appreciate all you're doing, really I do. But I can't."

He didn't much like it, but he had to respect her wishes, so he stayed where he was, feeling helpless. If there's one thing Jackson hated, it was feeling helpless. "Is there *anything* I can do for you?"

She shook her head. "Nothing." They sat there in silence for a while before she murmured, "It's all my fault."

"What are you talking about?"

"This wouldn't have happened if I hadn't taken out the restraining order."

"On my advice. So don't go blaming yourself."

"No. It was my decision. And it pushed him over the edge. Remember I told you that Ray wanted to do this legally, that he wouldn't endanger that? It was when he finally realized that he wasn't going to get any help from the law that he said screw it and took her anyway."

Something inside him sagged. She was right. Partly. But, dammit, she also wasn't right.

He rose, opened the blinds a little more and gazed out into the alleyway where a row of midsize cars rested under the carport roofing. "Vanessa," he said, his back to her, "blame is a waste of time. We have no way of knowing what pushed Ray over the edge. This might be all about Sharon, it might be her idea." He glanced over his shoulder. "Didn't you tell me you got the impression she was half-desperate?"

"She does nothing without Ray, trust me."

She looked so small, so cold. There was a deadness to her that terrified him. He wanted to comfort her, but she had a wall around her as thick as stone. She'd put it up on Friday night and it hadn't come down yet. It made him feel like he was being rejected, but he chastised himself for thinking about himself. He needed to cut her some slack. The woman's kid had been taken.

Turning, he dropped to one knee next to the bed, took her hand in his. "Look, I'm here." He ventured a small smile. "And I still love you, whether that's something you want to hear or not."

She met his gaze with those dead eyes. "Do you?"

"Very much."

She looked at their joined hands. "I'm sorry you do."

Her response felt like a knife in his gut. "What the hell does that mean?"

Slowly, sadly, she shook her head. "It's not going to work. You and me. It was good having you in my life. It was so wonderful having hope again. But it's not going to work."

He fought the urge to grab her by the upper arms and shake her. "Vanessa, stop this. You're in no shape to be making those kinds of statements."

"It's all my fault, for reaching too far," she said in a hollow voice. "I lost sight of my plan—to stay clean, to get educated and get my kids raised. I got to leaning on you, turning to you for advice, feeling protected and cared for. It was lovely, absolutely lovely. I listened when you advised getting the restraining order—I tried to act like a regular, law-abiding citizen, tried to play it by your rules. I tried to forget who I am and who you are. But it's no good, Jackson. Really, it isn't."

He stood, looked down at her, fear and anger waging a war inside. "Don't do this. Not now, when you're half-crazy with worry. Now is not the time to say things like this. We haven't slept, we're both on the edge here."

"Yes, I know." She gazed up at him with a poor attempt at a smile. "And of course we'll talk about it some more when—and if—I get Katy back. But it's so clear to me, Jackson. In some ways, I was better off without you."

That one really stung. "How can you say that?"

"Because I was better when I thought I had to do it all alone. It was empty, sometimes, and lonely, but the path was there, right in front of me. I knew where I was going. You made me forget, and I can't afford to do that. Not anymore. It's over."

It's over. The words hit him hard. He felt like someone had reached inside, grabbed his guts and hollowed him out.

He told himself not to take what she was saying as

the final word. Vanessa tended to head immediately for the dark side, to give up when it came to thinking the two of them could make it. But, under most circumstances at least, she was a reasonable, open woman. She would come around.

She had to.

Meantime, he had to find Katy. To show Vanessa she hadn't made a mistake allowing him into her life. That he could and would take care of her to the best of his ability.

A wave of despair hit him. Whatever the stats were, he knew they weren't good. The more time went on, the less likely they were to find Katy.

Where in the hell was Ray keeping her?

Chapter 10

Gray, overcast mornings were typical of this time of year. "June gloom," they called it in Southern California. Today the gloom had lasted into the afternoon, and as she walked along, head lowered, all of it looked gray to Vanessa: the dirty streets that somehow got overlooked by the city's street cleaners; overflowing garbage cans; sidewalks littered with discarded magazines, fast-food cartons, beer cans. The only brightness came from the outfits worn by the girls and women plying their wares—brief spandex halter tops and shorts, glittering four-inch heels. They stood on street corners and in alleyways, in groups and alone.

One girl sat on a bus stop bench, huge, heavy breasts pouring out of her low-necked top, lots of teased black hair. She wore a tiny short skirt, her legs spread just slightly, so you could see that she wore no underwear.

Vanessa had been one of these girls not so long ago, and the memories were overwhelming her already fragile emotional state. She recalled shivering with cold on winter nights, the not knowing if a john would be quick and easy or want more for his money. The ever-present potential for violence. The smells—the bad teeth, bad hygiene, cheap hair gel. The act she put on because she was more afraid of Ray than of any of the johns. Intimidation and fear had been her life for way too long.

How had she survived this? Where had she found the will to get clean and get out? Inner strength, they'd always told her, that was what had done it. Today there was no inner strength; today she was a mother in full desperation mode, and she was here because she had to do *something*.

Vanessa had firsthand knowledge of how Ray's mind worked. He was territorial, and he never really felt comfortable away from what he'd established as his personal terrain. She knew the police had been here, done their questioning, used their snitches. But maybe they'd missed something, she'd thought, so she had come back to the streets she'd vowed never to set foot on again.

She'd been here for two hours, had knocked on doors, asked questions, shown Katy's picture. All for nothing. She was a fool. Maybe she deserved what was happening to her for asking too much from life.

She stood still, shook her head. Stop it, she told herself. That was old thinking, the thinking that had kept her in a cocoon of drugs and johns and terror for too long. She knew better now, and she had to go on. Her kids needed her to go on.

The last of the hangouts from the old days was a rundown coffee shop with a long, coral Formica counter and a couple of rear tables. As she walked in, she didn't recognize any of the hookers taking a break here. After all these years most of them had moved on or died. AIDS, drugs, beatings.

Behind the counter she spotted the same waitress from the old days. What was her name? Melanie. Such a pretty name, Vanessa had always thought, for such a hard face. The same bright-red hair, the same penciled-in eyebrows, the small eyes, tall and skinny in her stained uniform. As always she wore a frown on her face. But underneath it all, there was unexpected kindness. Always an extra cup of coffee, a free doughnut here and there. For some, anyway. It took a while to get on Melanie's list, but when you were added to it, she looked out for you.

Vanessa sat. "Hey, Melanie."

She looked up from sponging off the countertop. "Yeah?" Her eyes widened and she stopped, stared. "Vanessa? That you?"

"It is."

"I thought you were dead," she said with her customary bluntness.

"I very nearly was."

The older woman studied her some more, then nodded, a hint of a smile on her hard face. "You're clean, aren't you."

"Nearly seven years."

"Wow, one of the ones that got out. Good for you."

Vanessa reached inside her purse for a picture of Katy. "This is my little girl, Katy."

Melanie took it, nodded. "How pretty. Oh, sweetie, I'm so glad for you. You had, what, a couple of other kids? Boys?"

"Yes, Shane and Thomas. Still got that amazing memory, don't you?"

"Some things just stick." She seemed to hesitate before asking, "How are they? They with you?"

"Yes. All three. I have a job, a real job too. We live in Venice."

Hand on hip, Melanie shook her head. "Wow, one of the ones that did it. You know, we got a group of girls, they come here sometimes on the sly, trying to think of how to get out. You could talk to them."

"Maybe I will sometime. But, listen, Melanie. Have you seen Ray?"

All the liveliness went out of her eyes. "Him. Used to see him all the time, busting in here, rounding up his chicks, making sure they got back out on the street. Been a while, though. I hear he's pretty full time dealing, gave up his little rent-a-girl sideline."

"So you haven't seen him in the last, say, two days?"

"No, sweetie. Why?"

Her eyes filled; she was amazed she had any more tears left. "He kidnapped my Katy and I'm trying to get her back."

"Oh, no." Melanie gripped her hand tightly before letting it go. "You got some more pictures? I'll pass them around, get people on it."

She brought out the rest of the stack, handed it to the waitress. She was done here; there was no more she could do.

"Thanks so much, Melanie." She grabbed a napkin, found a pen, scribbled her phone number on it. "Call me. When this whole thing is over, when I have my baby again, I'd love to come back, talk to those girls, give them some hope."

For the first time in Vanessa's memory, Melanie's eyes misted over. "I'll hold you to it."

When she walked in the door that evening, both boys came rushing over to her. Thomas hugged her, Shane stood nearby, not touching her, but she knew he wanted to.

"Mom, you're home," Thomas said. "I was so worried."

"I told you I'd be back, honey. Any word?"

He shook his head. "Not yet."

Lupe walked into the kitchen, one side of her face wrinkled, as though she'd been sleeping on it. "You had anything to eat?"

Vanessa shook her head. "Can't."

Her aunt grabbed her arm, brought her over to the table. "Sit. You eat and now. You need your strength for when Katy comes back."

For when Katy comes back. Right. She was bone weary, wishing again she had Lupe's faith and certainty that all would be well eventually. The soup her aunt put in front of her smelled wonderful, but her stomach rebelled. "Maybe some toast, Lupe?" she said, trying to work up a smile. "I just can't manage this."

"No problem."

Vanessa looked at the boys, stroked Thomas's still-hairless cheek. "I'm okay. Go, watch TV. I'm fine."

After a long look at her, they retreated to the living room again, and after she set some toast down in front of Vanessa, Lupe joined the boys.

She tried to eat some toast, letting the sound of the television lull her. Her head felt heavy, her neck unable to support the weight. She was nearly asleep when she heard a soft knocking on the back door.

She looked up, startled. Was she dreaming?

The knock came again. Quickly, she got up, went to the door, looked through the window.

It was night now, and in the light from the yellow bug bulb, she could see a woman wearing a scarf. Her face had been badly beaten—one side of her lip was swollen, there were bruises all over her face. It was Sharon.

Vanessa opened the door quickly, grabbed Sharon's arm. "Where is she?"

Sharon's eyes, one of which was red, its lid swollen, filled. "I'm so sorry."

"Has something happened to Katy? Is she all right?"

"Ray, he beat me. He beat me so bad."

She couldn't find an ounce of compassion for the woman at that moment. "Tell me, damn you. Where is she?"

The other woman sniffed, wiped a hand across her face. "I'll take you there."

Vanessa tightened her grip on Sharon's arm, squeezed with all her might. "Is she all right?"

"Yes." Sharon jerked her arm free, obviously annoyed. "That's why I'm here. I'll take you to her."

Relief, followed by a small kernel of hope, flooded her. "Okay. I need to just tell my family—"

"Don't say a word," Sharon interrupted. "Not to anyone."

Vanessa jerked a thumb toward the interior of the apartment. "But they're right here. They'll worry."

"No. Nothing. No family, no cops. Come with me now or forget it."

She hesitated. Could she trust her? Was this a trap?

As though she'd read her mind, Sharon said, "I'm done, Vanessa. I'm leaving him. But taking Katy wasn't right. I must have been crazy. I want to make it right."

"Why didn't you just bring her to me?"

"Ray, he, uh, chained her to the bed. He has the key."

"Oh, my God." Chained? To a bed?

Quickly she thought about her next move. Lupe was there, the boys would be okay. She had to take the chance.

"Okay. Let me get my purse." Without waiting for a response, she hurried back into the kitchen and grabbed her purse. On the way back to Sharon, she glanced around quickly, looking for weapon. There was a sharp knife, one used for cutting vegetables, lying next to the sink. Masking her actions by pretending to check something in her purse, she slipped the knife into a side pocket and joined Sharon Ortiz, waiting at the back door.

Jackson pulled up in front of The Last House on the Block, dashed out of the car and knocked on the door. It was after hours, but Mac had told him to meet him here. The door opened; Mac motioned him inside.

Jackson followed him to his desk. "What do you have for me, Mac?"

His old friend seemed to understand that there was no time for niceties and got right to it. "Someone I know is real good at hacking into computer systems. I have some information that might be helpful to you, but you don't get to ask me how I got it."

"Fine. What is it?"

"I had someone search all property owned by Ray Ortiz or his wife."

"Did that," Jackson said, raking his fingers through his hair distractedly. Exhaustion and tension were catching up to him as each hour dragged on without finding Katy. "Got the Encino place, an apartment near downtown and a Palm Springs condo. No one at any of them. No sign of their cars."

"And that's where my friend comes in. Remember, no questions."

"Are you nuts? I don't care if your guy can hack into the Pentagon. If you got something, I want it. This is Vanessa's child."

Mac nodded grimly. "Okay then, fine."

He took a sheet of paper from a top drawer in his desk. "Ortiz's mother lives in Montebello. Or *lived*— she's dead. It's a small house held under her maiden name, Beltran, and no one's owned it since. But the utilities are turned on. The phone, unlisted, is also under the mother's name. My source managed to find out who's been paying the bills, and it's Ortiz." He slid the paper across the desk. "Don't know if it will pan out, but at least it's something concrete."

Jackson snatched up the piece of paper. "I owe you big-time, Mac."

His friend's expression turned serious. "Find the little girl."

For the first part of the drive—in a beat-up old Chevy, which one of Ray's "associates" had supplied—Ray's wife had been filled with self-pity, dumping all her complaints on what she must have figured was someone who would commiserate. She whined about how she truly didn't know the kind of man she married, how he'd swept her off her feet, how he'd been so "sweet" when he was courting her. But Vanessa made no comments, none at all, and eventually Sharon seemed to understand that she wasn't interested. Her mind was too much on Katy to hear another person's tale of woe. So Sharon stopped talking, and silence filled the car.

Vanessa wasn't sure if Sharon was driving her to Katy or to her death, and at this point she nearly didn't care. It had all been too much to cope with, and with no sleep, she knew she wasn't thinking clearly. On top of that, the scene with Jackson early this morning kept reverberating in her head. It had been cruel to treat him that way, after all he'd done for her, for her family, practically from day one, when he'd helped her deal with Ray.

But deep inside she knew she was right. If she never got Katy back—and the thought opened up a pit of desolation so awful, it was hard to recover from it—then she would have enough to do taking care of her boys while grieving, without having to worry about all the compromises and adjustments necessary for two people from such different backgrounds.

Still, the look on his face—stricken, shocked, hurt—it wasn't a good picture to be carrying around all day.

And yes, perhaps she should have waited for another time, maybe after the police found her baby. Maybe she was doing something really stupid by sitting in the car with one of her child's kidnappers. But she was here now, and that was it.

Eventually they turned on to a small street of single-family homes, some of which looked old and shabby, others of which had been upgraded, second stories added, new paint and landscaping. Sharon pulled into the driveway of one of the nonupdated ones, with a much-repaired shingle roof, dusty, pale-peach concrete walls with white showing through in places, and grass that hadn't been mowed or watered in a while.

"Ray told me," Sharon informed her as she turned off the engine, "that he won't be back till late tonight, so it's okay. So it's up to you to figure out how to get the chains off Katy. I'm taking my bag and heading out. My parents hated Ray from the start, but I had to do something rebellious, right?" she said with self-disgust. "I had to be different from my sisters and their safe, boring husbands and safe, boring lives." She shook her head. "Always the loser, that's me."

Vanessa was barely listening; even though Ray's wife had said Ray wasn't at home, she looked around, still not sure this wasn't a trap. There were no other cars parked nearby, but she couldn't see what was behind the closed garage door. And yes, Sharon seemed sincere, but she could have been a superb actress, and this all could have been a plot to bring Vanessa here, away from her family and all potential help, and do away with her. In Ray's twisted mind, he could be figuring all he needed to do was tell a judge of his love for his little girl and his determination to lead a straight, clean life, and then full custody would be awarded to him and his wealthy wife.

She shook her head. She was tired, really tired, and needed to watch the fantasizing. As she followed Sharon into the house, she remained watchful. She also reached into her purse and palmed the small, sharp knife. If anyone came after her, she wouldn't go down without a fight.

Sharon unlocked the front door, calling out, "Ray?"

There was no answer, so she turned around to Vanessa and said, "See? He isn't here, so we're okay."

Which, Vanessa reminded herself again, either was or was not the truth.

They were in a small living room with stained gray carpeting and old, sad-looking furniture. An opening across the way led to the rear of the house, which was where Sharon headed now. "This used to be Ray's mom's house. I didn't even know about it until this… well, you know."

From her key chain, she chose another, newer key. She stopped at what seemed to be a bedroom door and turned the key in a padlock, then pushed the door open and entered.

Before following her, Vanessa braced herself for what or who was inside. Ray? One of his cohorts? Was it a trap or was her child on the other side of the door? And if she was, was she alive?

Holding tightly to the knife and keeping her gaze moving around as she did, she walked into the room. Right away she saw Katy. She was lying on a single bed with a headboard of iron rails, one small wrist chained to one of the rails. And she was very, very still.

"Oh my God," she cried and rushed over to her daughter.

"It's okay," Sharon said. "She's just sleeping."

But if she was just sleeping, why hadn't the sound of her mother's voice woken her? Vanessa put her arms under her child's body and brought her to her chest. Rocking her, she asked Sharon, "What did you do, drug her?"

"Just a little. She wouldn't stop crying for you. It was driving Ray crazy. He was gonna hit her to make her stop, but I told him I would give her one of my sleeping pills."

"A whole pill?"

"Two, actually. I mean, they hardly work on me at all, so I figured it would be fine."

Vanessa cautioned herself not to scream at this imbecile of a woman, who couldn't figure out that a child's smaller body weight would require a smaller dosage. As she spoke, she tried to keep her tone even because, as much of a fool as this woman was, at the moment she was an ally. She'd brought her here. "What was the name of the pill?"

When Sharon named a well-known opiate, Vanessa got scared. It was one of those you only got by prescription—she knew that because one of the girls at work told her about her mother's insomnia and how this "magic pill" had worked wonders.

Bracing her daughter with one arm, she used her free

hand to pull up one of Katy's lids. Her pupils seemed a normal size, which, she supposed, was something. And Katy's breathing was regular, but it seemed shallow to her...or was she imagining it? Carefully setting Katy back down, she rose from the bed.

"Are you sure you don't have the key?"

"Ray has it."

"Sharon, we have to get her to the hospital."

The other woman backed away, hands in front of her, palms out. "No. No, I can't. I told you no cops, and they'll get involved. I have to get to the airport while Ray is gone. I have to get out of here. Right now."

"Katy could die, Sharon."

The other woman shrugged; it was the helpless, hopeless shrug of a perennial victim. "I'm sorry. Really I am, but I have no choice."

She turned to go, but just then a voice yelled out, "Hey, Sharon?"

The sound of the front door slamming brought both women to a shocked standstill. "Ohmigod," Sharon whispered. "Ray's back."

"Hey, Sharon, where are you?"

"Answer him," Vanessa whispered, looking frantically around for a place to hide.

"In Katy's room," Sharon called out.

Thinking quickly, Vanessa put her index finger over her lips to indicate to Sharon that she shouldn't give her away, then she moved to stand behind the open door. The minute Ray walked through, she would go after him with the knife; she would bite him, scratch him, kick him. She had the element of surprise on her side, at least.

If Sharon was still willing to help her.

If she wasn't, then she and Katy—and probably Sharon, too—were all goners.

Vanessa kept eye contact with the other woman, pleading with her silently, hoping just the strength of a mother's love for her child would be enough to keep Sharon from giving her away.

Ray's footsteps drew nearer and nearer. "They got cops all over the streets in L.A. None of my guys wants to be seen with me. Even the nickel junkies are avoiding me. I can't do business. This sucks." From the other side of the open doorway, Vanessa could hear him ask his wife, whose eyes were wide with fear, "What? What is it?"

Instead of answering right away—not a good move, as Ray had supersharp instincts—Sharon backed into the room and Ray followed. Now Vanessa could see his back as he gazed at his wife. Figuring it was now or never, she leaped out and rammed the knife into Ray's back.

He let out a howl and turned around. When he saw her, the rage on his face matched any fury she'd seen on it, ever. He reached behind him, trying to get the knife out. "Sharon. Pull it out. Now!"

But Sharon had taken off and was no longer in the room.

Ray lunged for Vanessa, but she kicked him, landing a solid blow to his knee. After emitting another howl of pain, he somehow managed to grab her. It might have been her imagination, but she thought she heard the sound of sirens in the distance.

She had no idea if the location of the knife was going to kill him or maim him, but at the moment he seemed filled with all the strength that rage brings. She tried to shake herself loose from his iron grip, but he held on, pulled her close, put one hand around her neck, his thumb pressing on her windpipe. She pushed at him, hit him, but he squeezed, muttering every curse he'd ever called her, over and over again, squeezing harder and harder until she could feel herself blacking out.

Suddenly, through her dizziness, she was aware of hearing a loud thump, followed by a moan. Like that, the pressure on her neck was gone. Gasping for breath, Vanessa fell to the ground. The sirens were closer now. Black dots dancing before her eyes, she looked up to see Sharon, holding a large, cast-iron frying pan and staring down. Vanessa managed to angle her head enough to see Ray lying on the floor, blood pouring out of the back of his head, eyes staring sightlessly at the ceiling.

Ray Ortiz was dead. *Good,* she thought, wishing she'd done it herself.

And then blackness descended, rendering her unable to do anything at all.

When next she opened her eyes, it was to see the faces of Lupe and Thomas, hovering over her. Groggy and disoriented, she tried to take in her surroundings. She was in a hospital. Her throat was killing her, she had an IV in her arm, she was hooked up to machines.

Katy! she thought, but couldn't say it. Frantically she looked around the room, then at Thomas. As though he'd read her mind, her son grinned. "Katy's okay, Mom. They didn't even have to pump her stomach."

She licked around her mouth before miming, "Where is she?"

"In the children's ward," Lupe said. "Shane's with her."

"We've been taking turns," Thomas said proudly.

Vanessa closed her eyes, mouthing, "Thank God." When she opened them again, Lupe was tapping Thomas on the shoulder.

"Go. Tell the doctor your mother is awake." After Thomas ran out of the room, her dear aunt took her hand. "You'll see her soon, *hija*. She's fine, I promise."

She felt her eyes filling with tears. She hurt, all over, but mostly it was her throat. Not that she cared— Katy was okay!

"How long?" she mouthed.

"Have you been here?" When she nodded, Lupe said, "Since last evening. It's noon now. And you're going to be okay, too. It will take a while for you to get your voice back. Strained vocal cords, clogged windpipe, they had to go in there and stretch it."

Vanessa put her hand over her bandaged throat. Lupe smiled again. "But the doctors say there will be one hundred percent recovery, both of you. My prayers were answered."

She squeezed her dear aunt's hand, mouthing, "Thank you."

"For praying?"

"For everything."

The scene that greeted Jackson as he stood in the doorway to Vanessa's room made his heart leap. Lupe sat next to the bed, holding Vanessa's hand, murmuring softly. Vanessa was awake. He'd been told she would be fine but he'd needed to see it for himself.

"Knock, knock."

Both women looked over at him. Lupe jerked her head in his direction. "And this one," she told Vanessa. "He wouldn't leave you. I kept telling him to go home, get some sleep, but he wouldn't leave your side. He finally passed out on the chair."

"Don't make such a big deal out of it," he said easily, walking into the room. "I've slept in plenty of chairs."

"He's a good one, *hija*," Lupe said. "I think we should keep him around."

Obviously, Lupe had no idea about his and Vanessa's previous conversation. And now wasn't the time to bring it up.

The older woman rose, saying, "I'll leave you two alone." As she passed him on the way to the door, she winked at him.

He stood at the end of her bed, staring at her. It killed him to see her bruised face, the bandages around her throat, the paleness of her skin, the IV in her arm. Just killed him. But she was alive.

He put his hand on her foot, squeezed. "Hi." She nodded. "You can't talk at all, right?" She nodded again. "You're going to be okay." Another nod. "You'll be here another couple of days."

This time she didn't nod; instead she moved her head from side to side.

"Yes. No arguments."

Her mouth was set in a stubborn line, and he nearly

smiled. "Not now but a little later we need to go over what happened. Right now, though, you need to rest."

She shook her head, made a gesture with her hand. "Tell me," she mouthed.

"You mean what we have so far?" When she nodded, he said, "The wife said she came to get you so you could take Katy, then she was planning on heading back east. Ray came home early, you stabbed him, he choked you, Mrs. Ortiz thought he would kill you so she hit him over the head with a frying pan. Which, by the way is one of the favorite weapons of abused women, only most of them do it while the hubby's asleep."

That got just the hint of a smile out of her.

"That about right?" When she nodded, he said, "Good."

He came around to the side of the bed, sat on the chair recently vacated by Lupe. He took her hand, which was limp. "When I came into that room and saw Ray lying in a pool of blood, and then you with your eyes closed, lying so still, I got scared, Vanessa. Big-time. I'm so glad you're all right."

She nodded, then mouthed, "Katy, too."

"Yeah," he said, smiling back. "Katy, too."

As he gazed at her, he wanted to say, *Did you actually mean what you said yesterday, that we had no future together?*

But not now, of course. In his opinion she'd shown extremely bad timing—compounded by extremely poor judgment—in bringing it up when she had, and he would not further compound the sin by doing the same now. Lots of time for that kind of discussion, when she was all better.

And if she thought she was kicking him out of her life, she'd have one hell of a battle on her hands.

"Mommy, Mommy!"

Both their attention was drawn to the door of the room where Katy, in a small wheelchair being pushed by a nurse, bounced up and down, a huge grin on her face. Thomas and Shane followed right behind. "Look, Mommy, I'm in a wheelchair! It's so much fun!"

Vanessa struggled to sit up Jackson adjusted the bed for her instead. After leaping off the wheelchair, Katy came running over to her. "How are you, Mommy? They said you got a hurt throat."

Vanessa held her arms out, but the nurse grabbed Katy's hand. "You need to be careful," she said. "See that tube in Mommy's arm? It's giving her lots of vitamins and we don't want it to come out."

Katy nodded, her face serious. "Okay, I'll be very careful."

Gingerly she climbed onto the bed, laid her head down on her mother's chest and patted her shoulder gently. Her mother's eyes filled with tears; she closed them and held her child close. There was complete silence in the room. Jackson felt his throat clog with emotion, and knew he wasn't alone.

"*Hija,* there's a call for you."

Vanessa glanced up at Lupe, who handed her the phone, shrugged and walked out of the room.

She'd been home three days, had slept most of the time because of the pain meds she'd been prescribed, and was just now managing to whisper. Jackson had visited every day, had sat with her, held her hand, and filled her in on the progress of the case. Sharon was pleading self-defense in the murder charge, but her part in the kidnapping would be one of those matters the lawyers would be haggling over for a while.

Vanessa and Jackson hadn't really talked about anything important during his visits, but that conversation they'd had days ago, before Katy's return, had been hanging there between them, the elephant in the living room one more time.

She put the phone to her ear. "Hello?" she whispered.

"Vanessa? This is Lillian Rutherford."

She had little time to be shocked, because the older woman went right on. "I heard you had some trouble a few days ago. Your little girl got taken, which had to have been awful for you, but everything's okay now."

"Yes," she managed. "Thanks for asking."

"Now, I know you can't talk," Lillian said briskly, "so I'll do most of that. The reason I'm calling is—" she emitted a big sigh "—this isn't easy."

What wasn't easy? Vanessa wondered. Telling her to get out of her son's life? Didn't she know she'd pretty much already done that?

"See, Jackson called me, told me he wants to marry you, adopt your kids. And I told him he needed his head examined."

"What?" It came out a croak and it hurt.

"Exactly. See? We both know what's right here, don't we?"

Still in shock from the previous sentence about marriage and adoption, and before she had any time to react to the next one, she listened as the woman barreled on. "Well, whatever you think and I think, the ornery boy is going to do it his way, and he told me so in so many words. Told me he was going to marry you and adopt your kids, like I said. And told me how he expects me to act, and that I should get to know you better because you're a very special and very brave and very hardworking person, that once I did get to know you I would grow to love you."

Her head was spinning.

"And he said that he was prepared to never see me again if I gave him any trouble about it. His own mama, can you believe that?"

"Oh, Mrs. Rutherford," she managed to whisper.

"Call me Lillian, for heaven's sake. We're going to get very close, you and me," she said grimly, "so you might as well."

"We're what?"

"Well, I'm not about to lose my son, am I? Lost one already years ago. Lost Jackson's daddy, too. The boy's all I have left."

"But…he's blackmailing you."

"It's not the first time, is it?" she said with indignation. "When he was a child, he was best friends with Clayton Harlow, a farmer's boy? Big black family, lots of kids. He'd bring Clayton home and I'd put up a fuss and he'd say, 'Mama, Clayton is my friend and I expect you to be nice to him.' And then back in high school there was this girl, Geneva, you could tell she had some colored blood in her, and Jackson was mad about her and wouldn't hear anything against her. The boy has never given my opinions the time of day. So this isn't the first time. And you know what?"

"What?"

"I have to say, and I don't like admitting it, his instincts have always been good. That Clayton was the sweetest boy, so good to his mama, owns the biggest hardware store in town now. Married that old girlfriend of Jackson's, by the way, who is also a fine person. So you see, Jackson's taste in friends and girlfriends has always been good, after you get past the, well, you know…"

She did.

The older woman sighed again. "So he said I had to make an effort. 'Stretch my boundaries' were the words he used. So I'm stretching."

Despite everything, Vanessa actually felt sorry for the woman. She'd been backed against the wall and told to get rid of a deep, generations-old mind-set. It couldn't have been easy for her to admit it.

"So you gonna marry my son?" Lillian asked.

"I… I'm not sure."

"He said if you said that, to tell you that stereotypes go both ways, to remember how it was when you first met, and to think about that for a bit."

What? Vanessa shook her head to clear it. Then she got it. Of course. In the beginning she'd been deeply prejudiced against Jackson because she'd been certain he was a bully, a Southern bully, then a Southern cop bully. One with a body but no brain. She'd made assumption after assumption because of his accent, his profession, his build. The color of his skin. And she'd been proven wrong, hadn't she? Hadn't he kept surprising her with who he was, as an individual, instead of as a type?

"See?" Lillian went on. "Jackson also said you've had a difficult life and that one day you'd tell me about it. When I pressed, he said it was your business and no one else's, and that he was fine with all of it. His daddy always said that—a person's past was his past and only the way he acts in the present reveals the kind of man he is."

Vanessa's head continued to spin with shock and surprise. Not to mention, she thought wryly, that she'd had no idea, from their previous meeting, how much of a talker Jackson's mother was.

"Well, I've rattled on and on here," Lillian said now, as though reading her mind. "All I ask is you have some patience with me. I know I use some outmoded language, but I'm working on it. I hope you'll make my boy happy, Vanessa. He's deeply in love and, really, all I want is for him to be happy. You're a mother, so you know how that feels."

Yes she was, and yes she did.

"Thank you," she whispered. "This must have been difficult for you."

"You know what?" She chuckled. "After I got started, it wasn't so bad. 'Bye now."

He'd just stepped out of the shower and was rubbing a towel over his hair when he heard the doorbell ringing. Slinging the towel around his hips and tucking it in, he walked toward the door, wondering who in the hell would be visiting at seven in the morning.

He yanked it open. "Yeah?"

Vanessa stood there, dressed in green sweats, her face free of makeup, her hair back in a ponytail, her arms crossed over her chest and looking really, really pissed off.

She walked past him, right into the room, saying, "I have a bone to pick with you." It came out as a hoarse whisper.

"Do you?" He closed the door.

She whirled and faced him. "You told your mother that you wanted to marry me and adopt my children."

He set his chin. "And I meant every word. You got a problem with that?"

She pointed her index finger at him and closed the gap between them, aiming for his chest. "Yes, I have a problem with that. The problem is—" she poked him, hard "—you never bothered to ask me. Isn't that kind of backward?"

"I assumed you knew."

One black eyebrow arched up. "I was supposed to read your mind?"

He'd been readying himself for a marathon battle, but with that sentence, something tight and scared inside him that he'd been holding on to for days suddenly let down as it dawned on him. She was teasing him!

Grinning like a fool, he grabbed both her hands and pulled them around his waist, then hugged her tightly. She hugged him back. He drank her in, the feel of her, the smell of her. Eyes closed, they stood that way for quite a while. He didn't ever remember feeling this happy, this contented, this *right*.

Finally Vanessa pulled her upper body away, keeping

her arms around him while she gazed up at him. "That's some mother you have there," she whispered.

"I hope she didn't insult you."

"Not really. But you held her hostage, Jackson. That's not nice to do to the woman who raised you and loves you so deeply."

"And I'd do it again. I wanted you to know that whatever influence she had on me never stopped me from doing what I thought was right. I really needed you to know that, Vanessa."

"I got it." She cocked her head to one side. "How come you never told me about Clayton and Geneva?"

That one confused him. "What about them?"

"That your history is not only about all-white friends and girlfriends?"

"Did Mama tell you about them?" He shrugged. "What, was I supposed to assure you of my lack of prejudice by saying 'Some of my best friends are—'?" He shook his head. "We both got lots of stories to tell each other. And years to do so. The thing is, *will* you marry me?"

He held his breath. This was, after all, the big issue.

She continued to gaze at him for a while, then dropped her grip on his waist. "Can you imagine me and my brood visiting your small town in Alabama?"

"Yes, I can."

Her expression turned deadly serious. "People will talk."

"Some will, yeah. And in case you weren't aware, there is no more prejudice in Alabama than there is in L.A. Just comes out different, is all, and whatever it is, we'll deal with it."

She considered this, walked over to his bookshelves. She traced a finger along the spines, then looked at him again. "And what if we don't make it?"

"We will."

"But what if we don't, and my kids think of you as their dad and get their hearts broken?"

He moved toward her. "I'm not going to answer that question."

"Why? Don't want to face the possibility?"

"No, because I don't have a crystal ball. Could we not make it? Sure. Do I think we won't? I'm pretty sure we'll make it just fine."

He drew her into his arms, gazed down on her. "I love you, Vanessa Garner. Do you love me?"

Those eyes of hers. God, they got to him. So clear, such a beautiful color. And at present so filled with both hope and fear. "You know I do."

"Say it."

"I love you, Jackson Rutherford."

Smiling, he drew her to him. "We'll have our battles, darlin', but we'll talk it out, just like we've done from the start. We're so good together, Vanessa, you know we are. And all those doubts of yours? It's just that old fear coming up again. Take a chance. Marry me, let me be your kids' daddy."

He kissed her then, put all the love and longing in his heart into it, and, as she always did, Vanessa responded.

Big-time. Lots of tongue and passion.

She pulled his towel away and took him in her hand. She knelt before him, kissed him softly where she held him and gazed up at him, love and trust shining from her eyes. "I knew I was done for, the minute I walked in here and all you had on was a towel. You fight dirty, Jackson."

"Hey, whatever it takes."

"Flowers. Phone calls. Protecting me from Ray. Adopting my kids. Your mama calling me." She shook her head, kept her gaze on him, all the while stroking his growing erection. "And even though I hate to honor anyone who fights so dirty, I will marry you. On one condition."

He felt his breathing growing harsh. "What?" he managed.

"That you take me to bed. Right now."

He swooped her up in his arms. "Talk about fighting dirty. This about kills me, but if you insist."

As he carried her to the bed, he heard her laughter—the whispered croaking version—and it filled his heart. And he knew that, together, they would make a home of their own. There would be some problems and some adjusting, some fighting and miscommunication. But, oh, the fun they would have making up. And, oh, the life he would have from now on, with Vanessa and her brood filling the days with joy.

Didn't get much better than that, now, did it?

* * * * *

Mediterranean Nights

Join the guests and crew of Alexandra's Dream,
the newest luxury ship to set sail on the
romantic Mediterranean, as they experience
the glamorous world of cruising.

A new Harlequin continuity series
begins in June 2007 with
FROM RUSSIA, WITH LOVE
by Ingrid Weaver

Marina Artamova books a cabin on the luxurious
cruise ship Alexandra's Dream, when she finds
out that her orphaned nephew and his adoptive
father are aboard. She's determined to be reunited
with the boy...but the romantic ambience of the ship
and her undeniable attraction to a man she considers
her enemy are about to interfere with her quest!

Turn the page for a sneak preview!

Piraeus, Greece

"THERE SHE IS, Stefan. *Alexandra's Dream*." David Anderson squatted beside his new son and pointed at the dark blue hull that towered above the pier. The cruise ship was a majestic sight, twelve decks high and as long as a city block. A circle of silver and gold stars, the logo of the Liberty Cruise Line, gleamed from the swept-back smokestack. Like some legendary sea creature born for the water, the ship emanated power from every sleek curve—even at rest it held the promise of motion. "That's going to be our home for the next ten days."

The child beside him remained silent, his cheeks working in and out as he sucked furiously on his thumb. Hair so blond it appeared white ruffled against his forehead in the harbor breeze. The baby-sweet scent unique to the very young mingled with the tang of the sea.

"Ship," David said. "Uh, *parakhod*."

From beneath his bangs, Stefan looked at the *Alexandra's Dream*. Although he didn't release his thumb, the corners of his mouth tightened with the beginning of a smile.

David grinned. That was Stefan's first smile this afternoon, one of only two since they had left the orphanage yesterday. It was probably because of the boat—according to the orphanage staff, the boy loved boats, which was the main reason David had decided to book this cruise. Then again, there was a strong possibility the smile could have been a reaction to David's attempt at pocket-dictionary Russian. Whatever the cause, it was a good start.

The liaison from the adoption agency had claimed that Stefan had been taught some English, but David had yet to see evidence of it. David continued to speak, positive his son would understand his tone even if he couldn't grasp the words. "This is her maiden voyage. Her first trip, just like this is our first trip, and that makes it special." He motioned toward the stage that had been set up on the pier beneath the ship's bow. "That's why everyone's celebrating."

The ship's official christening ceremony had been held the day before and had been a closed affair, with only the cruise-line executives and VIP guests invited, but the stage hadn't yet been disassembled. Banners bearing the blue and white of the Greek flag of the ship's owner, as well as the Liberty circle of stars logo, draped the edges of the platform. In the center, a group of musicians and a dance troupe dressed in traditional white folk costumes performed for the benefit of the *Alexandra's Dream*'s first passengers. Their audience was in a festive mood, snapping their fingers in time to the music while the dancers twirled and wove through their steps.

David bobbed his head to the rhythm of the mandolins. They were playing a folk tune that seemed vaguely familiar, possibly from a movie he'd seen. He hummed a few notes. "Catchy melody, isn't it?"

Stefan turned his gaze on David. His eyes were a striking shade of blue, as cool and pale as a winter horizon and far too solemn for a child not yet five. Still, the smile that hovered at the corners of his mouth persisted. He moved his head with the music, mirroring David's motion.

David gave a silent cheer at the interaction. Hopefully, this cruise would provide countless opportunities for more. "Hey, good for you," he said. "Do you like the music?"

The child's eyes sparked. He withdrew his thumb with a pop. *"Moozika!"*

"Music. Right!" David held out his hand. "Come on, let's go closer so we can watch the dancers."

Stefan grasped David's hand quickly, as if he feared it would be withdrawn. In an instant his budding smile was replaced by a look close to panic.

Did he remember the car accident that had killed his parents? It would be a mercy if he didn't. As far as David knew, Stefan had never spoken of it to anyone. Whatever he had seen had made him run so far from the crash that the police hadn't found him until the next day. The event had traumatized him to the extent that he hadn't uttered a word until his fifth week at the orphanage. Even now he seldom talked.

David sat back on his heels and brushed the hair from Stefan's forehead. That solemn, too-old gaze locked with his, and for an instant, David felt as if he looked back in time at an image of himself thirty years ago.

He didn't need to speak the same language to understand exactly how this boy felt. He knew what it meant to be alone and powerless among strangers, trying to be brave and tough but wishing with every fiber of his being for a place to belong, to be safe, and most of all for someone to love him....

He knew in his heart he would be a good parent to Stefan. It was why he had never considered halting the adoption process after Ellie had left him. He hadn't balked when he'd learned of the recent claim by Stefan's spinster aunt, either; the absentee relative had shown up too late for her case to be considered. The adoption was meant to be. He and this child already shared a bond that went deeper than paperwork or legalities.

A seagull screeched overhead, making Stefan start and press closer to David.

"That's my boy," David murmured. He swallowed hard, struck by the simple truth of what he had just said.

That's my *boy*.

"I CAN'T BE PATIENT, Rudolph. I'm not going to stand by and watch my nephew get ripped from his country and his roots to live on the other side of the world."

Rudolph hissed out a slow breath. "Marina, I don't like the sound of that. What are you planning?"

"I'm going to talk some sense into this American kidnapper."

"No. Absolutely not. No offense, but diplomacy is not your strong suit."

"Diplomacy be damned. Their ship's due to sail at five o'clock."

"Then you wouldn't have an opportunity to speak with him even if his lawyer agreed to a meeting."

"I'll have ten days of opportunities, Rudolph, since I plan to be on board that ship."

* * * * *

Follow Marina and David as they join forces to uncover the reason behind little Stefan's unusual silence, and the secret behind the death of his parents....

Look for From Russia, With Love
*by Ingrid Weaver
in stores June 2007.*

REQUEST YOUR FREE BOOKS!

2 FREE NOVELS PLUS 2 FREE GIFTS!

Silhouette® Romantic

SUSPENSE

Sparked by Danger, Fueled by Passion!

YES! Please send me 2 FREE Silhouette® Romantic Suspense novels and my 2 FREE gifts. After receiving them, if I don't wish to receive any more books, I can return the shipping statement marked "cancel." If I don't cancel, I will receive 4 brand-new novels every month and be billed just $4.24 per book in the U.S., or $4.99 per book in Canada, plus 25¢ shipping and handling per book plus applicable taxes, if any*. That's a savings of at least 15% off the cover price! I understand that accepting the 2 free books and gifts places me under no obligation to buy anything. I can always return a shipment and cancel at any time. Even if I never buy another book from Silhouette, the two free books and gifts are mine to keep forever.

240 SDN EEX6 340 SDN EEYJ

Name	(PLEASE PRINT)
Address	Apt. #
City	State/Prov. Zip/Postal Code

Signature (if under 18, a parent or guardian must sign)

Mail to the **Silhouette Reader Service™:**
IN U.S.A.: P.O. Box 1867, Buffalo, NY 14240-1867
IN CANADA: P.O. Box 609, Fort Erie, Ontario L2A 5X3

Not valid to current Silhouette Intimate Moments subscribers.

Want to try two free books from another line?
Call 1-800-873-8635 or visit www.morefreebooks.com.

* Terms and prices subject to change without notice. NY residents add applicable sales tax. Canadian residents will be charged applicable provincial taxes and GST. This offer is limited to one order per household. All orders subject to approval. Credit or debit balances in a customer's account(s) may be offset by any other outstanding balance owed by or to the customer. Please allow 4 to 6 weeks for delivery.

Your Privacy: Silhouette is committed to protecting your privacy. Our Privacy Policy is available online at www.eHarlequin.com or upon request from the Reader Service. From time to time we make our lists of customers available to reputable firms who may have a product or service of interest to you. If you would prefer we not share your name and address, please check here. ☐

SRS07

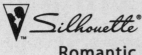

ROMANTIC
SUSPENSE

Sparked by **Danger,**
Fueled by **Passion.**

*This month and every month look for
four new heart-racing romances
set against a backdrop of suspense!*

Available in June 2007

Shelter from the Storm
by **RaeAnne Thayne**

A Little Bit Guilty
(*Midnight Secrets miniseries*)
by **Jenna Mills**

Mob Mistress
by **Sheri WhiteFeather**

A Serial Affair
by **Natalie Dunbar**

Available wherever you buy books!

Visit Silhouette Books at www.eHarlequin.com   SRS0507

Silhouette® Romantic SUSPENSE

COMING NEXT MONTH

#1467 SHELTER FROM THE STORM—RaeAnne Thayne
He was responsible for her father's downfall and must now work with the woman he's long desired to save a young girl from a vicious crime ring. As they move forward with the case, his secret could endanger their victim—and his heart.

#1468 A LITTLE BIT GUILTY—Jenna Mills
Midnight Secrets
Their attraction has been building since the moment they were assigned to capture a murderer. But when he discovers that she's been hiding a secret agenda that threatens his career, he must decide what's more important: exploring a potential love interest...or revenge.

#1469 MOB MISTRESS—Sheri WhiteFeather
When a Texas-bred cowboy discovers he's the prized grandson of an infamous mob boss, he must come to terms with his new identity while resisting the allure of the mysterious woman claiming to know the dark secrets of his past.

#1470 A SERIAL AFFAIR—Natalie Dunbar
Special Agent Marina Santos gets an unexpected surprise when she's assigned to work with her ex-love, Lt. Reed Crawford. Neither is happy to see the other, but both must overcome their grudges to catch a serial killer...even if it rekindles a spark they weren't prepared for.